DEATH NOTE
デスノート

L

change the WorLd

written by
M

Translated by
Takami Nieda

VIZ MEDIA
SAN FRANCISCO

DEATH NOTE

L

change the WorLd

c o n t e n t s

L change the WorLd © 2007 M / 2008 "L" PLOT PRODUCE
All rights reserved.
First published in Japan in 2007 by SHUEISHA Inc., Tokyo.
English translation rights arranged by SHUEISHA Inc.

Art by Takeshi Obata
Original book design by chutte

English translation © VIZ Media, LLC

Published by
VIZ Media, LLC
P.O. Box 77010
San Francisco, CA 94107

www.viz.com

Library of Congress Cataloging-in-Publication Data

M.
[L, change the world. English]
Death note : L, change the worLd / written by M ; translated by Takami Nieda.
p. cm.
ISBN 978-1-4215-3225-7
[1. Bioterrorism--Fiction. 2. Terrorism--Fiction. 3. Mystery and detective stories.] I.
Nieda, Takami. II. Title. III. Title: L, change the worLd. IV. Title: Change the world.
PZ7.M11De 2009
[Fic]--dc22
2009016555

Printed in China
First printing, October 2009
Eleventh printing, August 2022

L

change the WorLd

written by M

Cast of Characters

L	Detective
Kimihiko Nikaido	Immunologist
Maki	Nikaido's daughter
Kimiko Kujo	Nikaido's assistant
Hideaki Suruga	FBI agent
Daisuke Matoba	Director of NPO Blue Ship

ℒ272 LA (L's Affair)

"So how's it going, Fairman? Must be difficult having to step in for Naomi and all."

FBI agents Sugita and Fairman managed to avoid the L.A. traffic as they headed down Vine Street toward the airport. In an effort to break the ice with Fairman, with whom he was partnered for the first time, Sugita brought up the subject of Naomi Misora, who'd left the Bureau the week before to get married.

By "difficult," Sugita was of course alluding to, among other things, Fairman's having to succeed an agent who had been stuck with the name "Misora Massacre." The agent who had earned L's trust.

"Difficult, yeah," Fairman replied laconically from the passenger seat. Perhaps not one for conversation.

"This is going to be one quiet ride," Sugita mumbled to himself. He rubbed the stubble on his face and looked down at the attaché case on Fairman's lap.

"What does the secretary of state want with confidential files from over twenty years ago anyway?"

"Who knows?" Fairman said. "Far be it for us foot soldiers to understand what the higher-ups are thinking, and most of the time it's safer that way."

Sugita noticed something and peered into the rearview mirror.

"What is it, Sugita?" Fairman asked.

"It's...nothing," said Sugita, shaking his head and getting a grip on the steering wheel.

"Sorry, man, I have to hop out for some cigarettes."

Sugita stopped for a red light and Fairman suddenly got out, attaché case in hand.

"Hey, the attaché case—"

Maybe he hadn't heard Sugita. But Fairman was not looking in the direction of the storefronts; instead he was looking at the street traffic as if waiting for something.

The cell phone inside Sugita's breast pocket vibrated. The display read "Private Call." Sugita hit the "talk" button.

"There are no patrons in the boutique, Sugita."

The voice was distorted by a vocoder. The call was ended before Sugita could even ask who it was.

"What was that? A wrong number?" Sugita mumbled to himself.

The moment Sugita turned his attention out the window, Fairman fired his gun. A tractor trailer crossing the intersection jerked out of control, then flipped over. The trailer slid on its side, sparks flying and black smoke pouring from the cab as it hurtled toward Sugita's car.

From around the curtain of smoke, a chase car closed in on Sugita from behind.

"Damn! We *were* being followed!"

Chewing his lip, Sugita tried to back the car into a side alley but was blocked. For a split second Fairman's sneering face came into view. His retreat cut off, Sugita glanced around for another escape.

"Got it!"

Sugita pointed the car toward the sheet of flame now engulfing the still-moving trailer and floored it. He jerked the wheel to avoid a collision and popped up onto the sidewalk, hitting a fire hydrant. The car picked up speed and smashed into the show window of a boutique. Sugita shouted, "There better not be any patrons!" as he tore into the store.

The trailer collided with the chase car and exploded. The doors flew open and the passengers, more flame than men, tumbled out onto the street.

"What do you think you're doing, Fairman?" Sugita bolted out of the boutique, still tangled in the dresses from the display racks, and marched up to Fairman, his gun drawn.

Fairman pointed his gun at Sugita, glanced at the burning men on the ground, and muttered in disgust, "The plan was to make it look like you burned to death along with the files, but—"

Fairman, who'd been inching backward, suddenly broke into a run. Sugita chased after him, but the streets were too crowded with onlookers to discharge his weapon.

Damn! Naomi up and quits and one day later this is what happens!

Fairman rounded a corner and collided with a guy in a bear suit standing in front of a crepe truck marked BEAR'S CREPES. The impact sent the bear's armful of soda bottles rolling down the sidewalk. Fairman slipped and fell as if a rug had been pulled out from under him.

Despite hitting his hip on the pavement, Fairman recovered quickly, retrieved the briefcase, and took off again.

"Mister, would you like a crepe?" the man in the bear suit called out casually as Sugita darted past.

"Not now. In a hurry!"

"They're good," the bear shouted. "And sweet!"

Fairman was moving slower after his fall. Then he crashed into an old woman, and they fell into a heap with her on top.

"Don't move!" Sugita raised his gun.

Fairman wrapped an arm around the old woman's neck and jammed the barrel of his gun up against her temple. The attaché case hit the ground nearby. The closest pedestrians ran for cover, while those across the street stood and watched.

The man in the bear suit distanced himself from the crowd and spoke in a low voice. A transceiver was embedded inside the costume.

"Watari, we have an unforeseen situation. Change target from the briefcase to the man on the run."

"Copy." Watari, looking down over the action from a nearby rooftop, peered through the scope of the rifle and mumbled, "Who do we have here?"

A little girl standing in front of a store with a Coke reached for a roll of Mentos, dropped a few of the candies into the bottle, and aimed it at Fairman. The Coke spurted like a geyser, squarely hitting its target. The barrel of Fairman's gun strayed from the old woman's neck for split second. Without missing a beat, Sugita put a bullet through Fairman's shoulder. In the same instant Watari took aim at the briefcase and squeezed the trigger. The briefcase burst apart, sending fiery fragments of classified documents flying like confetti.

Sugita surveyed the scene, unable to grasp what had happened.

"Respect your elders!" The girl with the Coke bottle scolded Fairman in rapid-fire Japanese, then walked away with a satisfied air.

Sugita stood in a daze, the charred documents in his hand, when the phone in his breast pocket vibrated. It was headquarters.

"Y286, we have an emergency! The orders we received from the secretary of state were faked. You might be in for an ambush."

"That you, Raye? Thanks for the intel. You might have saved my ass."

No sooner had he ended the call than the phone vibrated again. It was Naomi this time.

"I guess married couples think alike."

"What are you mad about? Listen, I can't seem to get ahold of Fairman. There's an assignment I forgot to tell him about."

Sugita watched the police car take Fairman away and let out a deep sigh. "Naomi, it looks like I'll be taking over your assignments."

"Why? What's going on?" she asked, suspicious.

Sugita replied as if throwing up his hands in surrender. "I'll take care of everything. The daily battles with the boss, the investigation with L, all of it. Congratulations on your nuptials, Naomi."

†

The young girl who'd thrown the Coke stopped at the crepe truck and stared at the bear mascot with the rounded shoulders. She took it upon herself to voice an honest opinion: "What a weird-looking crepe shop."

"Mind your own business," the man in the bear suit answered indignantly, and in Japanese.

The girl wasn't at all shocked to hear her native language in a foreign land. "Oh, you speak Japanese. Good. I'll have a chocolate crepe. Extra chocolate!"

Overwhelmed by the girl's energy, the man in the bear suit awkwardly began to make a crepe. The girl seemed satisfied when he handed her a crepe dripping with chocolate sauce.

"Ooh, that's plenty. But you know, you really should work on your crepe-making skills. See ya!"

The girl waved and strode off in high spirits.

The man in the bear suit lowered the zipper, shedding the suit down to his waist, and sighed.

"I'm no good with girls."

"It appears that even L isn't accustomed to dealing with such a cheerful girl," said Watari. The elderly gentleman approached with a serene smile and a rifle, which seemed incongruous with his butler-like comportment.

"That went well, Watari."

An attaché case exactly like the one Fairman carried rested at the feet—well, the bear paws—of the man called L.

"Classified FBI files; a valuable acquisition. I suppose this is a fair reward considering we helped the FBI flush out a spy in their midst."

L had switched the real attaché case with a dummy containing explosives and burned documents when Fairman had tripped and fallen. At the precise moment Sugita shot Fairman, Watari had destroyed the attaché case. For Detective L, this was a customary method of gathering intelligence.

"Are the contents what you were expecting?"

Watari's question seemed premature considering that L had just removed the thick report from the briefcase. However, like a child throwing a tantrum, he began to tear through the pages and in a blink of an eye had finished and was nodding emphatically.

"Yes. It reveals the truth behind the explosion of an infectious disease lab in 1980. The research lab was destroyed to conceal the biohazard linked with the development of a biological weapon."

A limousine pulled up next to the crepe truck. Watari stowed the rifle in the trunk and took out an enormous silver tray, complete with a domed lid. He removed the lid to offer L a *macaron* by Jean-Paul Hevin from the pyramid stack on the tray.

"But I don't believe the United States is developing virus weapons, at least not openly," Watari said, holding out the tray for L.

L snatched up four macarons, one between each of his fingers, and then quickly put one in his mouth as if he might devour his hand along with it.

"Yes, ever since Nixon's proclamation in '69, the U.S. has ceased all development of offensive biological weapons," he said, his mouth full, "and in theory have only been working on developing defensive weapons."

As if the macarons were not sweet enough for his taste, L twisted off the cookie top of one of them and drizzled chocolate sauce over it.

"Even nuclear weapons are in reality more effective as a deterrent than as an offensive weapon. By the same principle, the pretext of developing biological weapons as leverage to deter an attack would hold up. The former Soviet Union also secretly continued its biological weapons program even after signing the Biological Weapons Ban Treaty in '72. By the way—" Licking the chocolate from his fingers, L directed his gaze toward the park across the street. "Interesting girl."

The girl had befriended an old woman and her dog, and was now chasing after the dog as it wagged its tail playfully.

"Maki Nikaido." Watari smiled.

"Do you know her, Watari?"

"I know her father well. He is the world's preeminent immunologist, Professor Nikaido."

"He's listed as a distinguished professor at Wammy's, if I'm not mistaken."

Watari, also known as Quillish Wammy, had used the enormous earnings from the patents of his many inventions to establish the Wammy Foundation, an organization dedicated to building orphanages around the world.

Among them, one orphanage took in highly intelligent children from around the world without regard to nationality, race, or gender and provided them with a specialized education. The orphanage was called Wammy's House.

There was no formal school or academic departments at Wammy's. Instead, university professors, researchers, and top specialists in their fields from around the world were invited to give individual instruction to the children according to their abilities and potential.

"No doubt she's here with her father for the conference on infectious disease at the International Convention Center," Watari said.

L bit his nails as he watched the girl frolic with the dog. "I have a feeling we'll see her again."

"You're usually right about these things."

"And please include that agent in the list of candidates. The way he evaded the tractor trailer along with his presence of mind in minimizing fire damage by breaking open the fire hydrant was first rate."

"That was FBI agent Sugita. Agent Naomi Misora has left the Bureau," said Watari.

L began to climb out of the bear suit. "Our job is done here, Watari. We need to move on to the next mission immediately."

"Is there a case that might warrant your attention?"

"None of the police or investigative bureaus have recognized it as a case yet, but there have been reports of perpetrators of heinous crimes turning up dead of heart failure. Included among them are criminals whose whereabouts only I can verify," L said. "If this turns out to be a matter for further investigation, our old approach will not be effective. It's imperative that we get to work immediately."

"We should go to your personal safe house in Arizona. I'll arrange for a helicopter immediately. And what shall I do with these documents?"

Despite the trouble they'd gone through to obtain them, the confidential FBI files were no longer of importance to L.

"What's Near doing now?"

"Working on a white jigsaw puzzle at the House as usual. He did complain that the solution to the Madrid serial murders was too easy, too boring."

"Then pass these on to him. The attempted theft of these files is somehow connected with whoever is pulling Fairman's strings and the biohazard at the research lab. No doubt they were secretly exerting some influence over the 1980 presidential election as well. I would think finding the key to solve these mysteries is a perfect puzzle for him to work on."

"Of course. Now, shall we go?" Watari opened the limousine door and urged L inside. Shuffling toward the limousine with both hands shoved in his pockets, he stopped for a moment to look up at the sky. Watari loaded the bear suit into the truck. Straightening his rounded back just a bit, L uttered something like a premonition.

"If this turns out to be a murder case, we may be in for a long battle."

†

"I heard the commotion outside. Did something happen, Maki?" Professor Nikaido asked his daughter as he entered the hotel room.

"No, not really." Maki shook her head with an impish grin as Nikaido gently rested a hand on her head.

"Maki, I'm afraid I'm going to have to leave for Africa right away."

"Africa? What for?"

"Well, I received word from an immunologist friend of mine about an outbreak of an unknown virus in a remote part of the Congo. Two villages have been destroyed by an Ebola-like hemorrhagic fever. I know we made a promise to go to the original Disneyland after the conference…" He allowed the words to trail off apologetically. Maki frowned and shook her head.

"Daddy! People are suffering from the virus. What is it you have to do?"

Smiling grimly at his daughter's counsel, Nikaido patted her head. "You're right. I can't lose sight of what I have to do. It's what I've always been telling you, isn't it?"

"Daddy, I'm going with you," Maki declared.

"Now Maki, it's dangerous where I'm going. You're going back to Japan."

"I told you, I made a promise to Mom that I would take care of you in her place. That's what *I* have to do."

ℒ23 Fate

"Your room service is here, Ryuzaki. Tonight we have *Kototoi dango* from Mukoujima—"

Watari, mimicking a hotel waiter, wheeled in a cart and noticed that something wasn't right. The sweets piled high on the table, which L would normally devour in one sitting, remained untouched.

"Is something the matter, Ryuzaki?"

The Death Note, which was supposed to be under lock and key, lay open in front of L, who was staring intently at it.

"Kira and I have a score to settle. Too many people have lost their lives already." L held up the Death Note with the edge pinched between his fingers and pointed to the open page. "This is the last name to be written in the Death Note."

—L. Lawleit will die quietly of a heart attack twenty-three days from this date.

L's real name—the one only L and Watari knew—was unmistakably written in L's own hand.

Watari started to open his mouth but stopped and closed his eyes to contain his feelings. He would accept L's every decision and support him however possible. That was what he had resolved to do the very first time he met L at the time of the Winchester Mad Bombings when an eight-year-old L had prevented the outbreak of World War III.

Watari was well aware that L would analyze the facts objectively and determine for himself what he must do at every turn. If he came to the conclusion that there was only one move to get him to checkmate, then he would choose it without hesitation. Even at the expense of his own life. At the same time, L recognized that his life and work had saved countless lives. (If that sounds melodramatic, then perhaps countless people were spared from early deaths.)

And yet, this was the choice L had made. How could Watari object? And besides, the fate inscribed in the Death Note could not be reversed no matter what anyone said or did.

Suppressing all emotion, Watari uttered quietly, "So it's twenty-three days later."

"Twenty-three days. Watari, from now on, you must safeguard the world with the other letters."

L reached for a snack as if a burden had been lifted from his shoulders.

"I don't know that any of them can take your place..." Watari shook his head and sighed.

L. At Wammy's House this letter did not signify the twelfth letter of the alphabet alone. It stood for "Last One." The one who stood alone, without a successor. L also stood for "Lost One," as in a child dropped from heaven by some omnipotent being.

Ever since the boy, barely eight years old, made his existence known as the peerless and unrivaled Detective L and had been given the power to dispatch the police and intelligence agencies of the world, it became the purpose of Wammy's House to find and nurture a child with the talent to follow in L's footsteps.

"We'll need to restructure at Wammy's as well."

Watari watched over the rounded back of L as the detective ate the dango and turned his thoughts toward a world after L. L would not only vanish from the world, but from Watari's own life.

L 19 Destroyed

An enormous glass pot filled with white sugar cubes sat on a low table. L picked out the cubes with his left hand and popped them in his mouth one at a time.

There were over fifty monitors set up in front of the sofa. Until yesterday, every one of them had displayed news and surveillance video from around the world, but having served their purpose, all the monitors were now black. Except one.

L was watching a Japanese television program. A celebrity divorce was being reported as a big scoop.

Just as L turned toward the monitor, there were sounds of hurried activity in the wings of the studio. The broadcast cut away to an emergency press conference being held by the Metropolitan Police Department. Following a few words from the superintendent of police, Soichiro Yagami took the microphone.

"We are pleased to report that the case in the matter of Kira's indiscriminate murder of criminals is closed. Kira will never commit another crime."

The conference room buzzed with excitement at the announcement, and questions flew from every direction.

"Does that mean you've arrested him? Or is Kira dead?"

"Can you explain how Kira was killing his victims?"

"Answer the question!"

With that single tantalizing claim, Soichiro Yagami ended the conference and left amid the press's clamoring for answers. The conference room was in an uproar.

L stared at the screen without any hint of emotion.

"So Kira...no. *Light* is dead."

L heard a voice ring out, though had anyone else been with him, they would have heard nothing. L did not appear to be shaken, however. It was because a grotesque non-human outline was silhouetted on the floor, a shadow blocking the light spilling from the open door of the room. Only a shinigami, a death god with the ability to pass freely through walls, was capable of entering L's suite without triggering the security system.

"The Death Note brought to this world by you, a shinigami..." There were actually two Death Notes next to L. Slowly he picked up one of them and brought it closer to the candle flame. The shinigami Ryuk, despite looking somewhat displeased, did not try to stop him.

"Aww, I was hoping you would find an interesting use for it. And I told you all the rules for it and everything."

"An interesting use...for this?" L looked up and gave Ryuk a hard look. His image was reflected in Ryuk's enormous eyes.

"I dropped this notebook in this world because all of us in the shinigami realm were bored. At least Light gave us a good show. I was hoping you would entertain us by finding an amusing use for it too," Ryuk said.

"There isn't anything amusing about killing people. Besides, I've already used the notebook." L opened the notebook and held it up pinched between his fingers. "I've written my own name in the Death Note. This will be the first and last time I will use it."

Bringing his face much too close to the notebook, Ryuk sniffed the pages and stared at the name.

"The name Light so desperately wanted to know. Who would've thought you would write it in the Death Note yourself?" Ryuk twisted the large mouth that extended to his ears and snickered, his sharply pointed teeth peeking out between his lips.

With the notebook in his hand, L was still, as if he'd forgotten that the shinigami was there.

Ryuk watched for a moment, and after a while, he twisted his body unnaturally and cracked his neck.

"You're really not going to use it? That's no fun." Uttering the same words he'd said when Light died, Ryuk flapped his wings windlessly and disappeared through the ceiling.

Then there was silence again. L continued to gaze at the notebook, biting his nails all the while.

⅃ 18-1 Suruga

"What's with the lax security?" Suruga said into the lens. After showing his face to the surveillance camera, he stepped inside the Kira Investigation Headquarters, head tilted.

The fingerprint recognition scans, retinal scans, metal detectors, and other security measures in place went unused as the door opened. Suruga didn't even have to show his FBI badge.

Following the guide lights along the walls, he boarded the elevator and descended four floors underground. Ahead, past the heavy gate, was the Operations Room, the nerve center of the Kira Investigation building. There was no sign of anyone, and the countless monitors in the center of the spacious room were turned off.

"I'm with the FBI, anybody here?" Suruga's voice echoed in the silence. The room was utterly quiet, without even the memory of the psychological tug-of-war against the diabolical Kira that had been waged within its confines.

Suruga reversed his steps, scratching his head, and there he was.

"Whoa!" Suruga jumped back at the proximity of the man who suddenly appeared behind him.

L stood stooped forward, staring at Suruga. A tangled mop of hair, a plain white long-sleeve shirt, and faded blue jeans. He appeared to have a severely curved posture and was not poised for an attack as

Suruga first feared. The most prominent feature among the various odd parts cobbled together to form his face were the black-rimmed eyes of a chronic insomniac.

"Who are you?" Suruga asked, keeping both his guard and distance.

"Call me Ryuzaki," the man said as he jumped onto the sofa. Perched with his legs folded tightly against his body, he reached for the few sugar cubes remaining in the bottom of what appeared to be a giant fish bowl.

"Are you for real?" Suruga had been told that L went by the name Ryuzaki while working inside the Kira Investigation Headquarters. Despite the irritation he felt at the lack of interest the man showed toward his arrival, Suruga studied the back of his rounded shoulders as if to appraise him.

That L never revealed his real name or face was common knowledge. L had not even shown his face to Naomi Misora, who had worked with him to solve the Los Angeles BB Murder Cases. Thus Suruga had no choice but to take him at his word. However, the man standing before him was a far cry from his image of the world's top detective.

"Uh, forgive me, but I'll be blunt. Are you really L?"

"Yes. I, too, am L." The man who called himself Ryuzaki answered obliquely as if to evade the question. However, the answer seemed to boost Suruga's confidence in the man. *As long as no one else is around, the first step is to insinuate myself into Ryuzaki's favor. Without revealing my intentions...* Suruga thought, as he cleared his throat and approached the man sitting on the sofa.

"Hideaki Suruga," he said. "I'm with the FBI. Raye and I came up through the academy together. And now I've taken over Naomi's duties. I was supposed to host their wedding reception too, but..." Suruga let slip, to which the man on the sofa turned around, finally showing an interest. Actually, only his head twisted around while the rest of him continued to face forward like a marionette with tangled strings.

"You're Suruga? With the FBI?" Peering through the tangled mop of hair, the man fixed his gaze on Suruga's forehead.

Although Suruga remained stone-faced as per the rules of undercover work, he was assaulted by a chill that made his hair stand on end. The FBI had issued him a fake ID, and any reference to his real name in records L was likely to hack into had been changed. All the necessary precautions had been taken.

*But what if he can see my real name...*Fighting back the thought, Suruga continued, "I came here to offer my gratitude. For avenging Raye's and Naomi's deaths by defeating Kira. Don't hesitate to let me know if there's anything I can do for you."

The man calling himself L continued to stare at Suruga, while one arm found its way into the fish bowl. Seeing his hand fumbling inside the empty fish bowl in vain, L suddenly jumped off the sofa with a look of shock. He peered under the sofa and crawled under the table on all fours, clearly in search of something. Crawling over the bundle of cables extending from the monitors, he continued onward, moving his long arms and legs in a herky-jerky motion.

What the hell? Suruga was rendered mute by the man's bizarre action; L reached the wall and stood up after bumping into various obstacles along the way.

With a quickness belying his curved posture, he pushed against the unadorned wall according to some unwritten formula. Then, what appeared to be a seamless wall opened up, revealing compartments one after the next. In the first compartment was stored more of the same white long-sleeve shirts and faded jeans he was wearing, the second held a stash of cell phones, and the next a collection of Misa Amane merchandise. All of the contents were meticulously arranged and organized.

Finally, the last compartment L opened was empty.

"We have a situation!"

"What is it? A new case?"

Suruga couldn't help leaning forward. Maintaining a stern look, L asked, "Would you mind running out to get me some sweet potato cake from Funawa?"

L 18-2 Anguish

That night at Nikaido Research Lab, located atop a hill on the outskirts of Tokyo, only its director Professor Nikaido and his assistant Kujo remained.

"Professor, is the work on the antidote complete?"

"Yes, it's done. Tomorrow I'll inform the Ministry of Health, Labour, and Welfare and hand the antidote over to them. If the virus and antidote should ever fall into the hands of terrorists, the world would come to an end. All too easily," Nikaido said. "I'm going to store the virus and antidote in separate deep-freeze containers as a precaution. Neither can be opened without a password and my biometric authentication."

"Excellent work, Professor," Kujo said, but her face was still grave.

"Thanks," Nikaido answered, distracted. It was a different reaction from the kind of satisfaction a scientist might feel after seeing his work come to fruition.

Kujo asked, "Is something bothering you?"

"I understand this work will save lives. Nevertheless, I have smuggled a level four virus into this lab. I can imagine the protests by the residents in the area, to say nothing of the denouncement from the Ministry of Health, Labour, and Welfare. Of course, I'm prepared for the fallout."

For a private research facility, Nikaido Research Lab was equipped with cutting-edge equipment; it was one of only a few infectious disease labs in Japan outfitted to handle level four viruses—those categorized as having the highest biohazard risk. Level four viruses, such as the Ebola virus and Marbug virus, had extremely high fatality rates, while a level four lab was a facility with the safety equipment to handle such high risk viruses. (To put it another way, it took a level four lab to contain a level four virus in the event of an accident.)

There was, however, one precondition that made the handling of such viruses possible: the surrounding public had to agree to take on the risk of infection. Certainly other biosafety level four labs existed in Japan. But none had been used as a level four facility due to the protests of residents living in the surrounding area. For the residents, it was an obvious and natural reaction to the threat of a virus as deadly as Ebola being brought into their neighborhood. Nikaido Research Lab was no exception; it was restricted from bringing in anything higher than a level three risk as spelled out in an agreement reached with the surrounding residents when the lab was built.

"But Professor, it isn't as if you conducted this research for fame or for personal gain."

"You're right. People are suffering as we speak, and yet the development of the antidote was stalled simply because there isn't enough of a market for it. Only developing countries are being affected by the virus. I merely wanted that to change. But…" Nikaido took a long look at the two ampules before him. "I don't have to tell you that the current strategy for the most part has been to treat the symptoms. There has never been an antidote as foolproof as this one. This virus is like a ticking time bomb that has a two-week incubation period, during which the viral cells multiply inside the host without their knowing they've been infected. Depending on how the virus is used, it could very well become the ultimate weapon."

The liquid contained inside the two ampules seemed to sparkle, as if spurning such a ghastly fate.

"Apparently Kira, who caused quite an uproar, was capable of killing anyone of his choosing. On the other hand, whoever comes in possession of this virus, and the antidote, would be capable of killing everyone but the people of his choosing. In that regard, the virus could turn out to be nastier than Kira if it were used in service to a dangerous ideology."

Nikaido sighed deeply and turned toward the picture frame on top of the desk. In it was a family picture capturing his happier days.

"This virus will not be the property of Japan alone. The Ministry of Health will likely decide to send it to the CDC. In the end, all I've done is led the way toward developing a virus weapon. What would my wife say if she were alive…" A self-loathing smile crept across Nikaido's face.

"But Professor, the U.S. has declared that it will only conduct biological weapons research for defensive purposes." Despite Kujo's best effort to put him at ease, the hard look on Nikaido's face remained.

"Daddy, dinner's ready!" Maki appeared wearing an apron.

"Maki, you came in here without my permission again, didn't you? I'll have to have a talk with the security guard," Nikaido said. Though his tone was disapproving, Nikaido was smiling.

"Okay, okay, but come home before dinner gets cold. And how long have you been wearing that same lab coat? Off with it already!" No sooner had she spoken than Maki was at her father's side, pulling off Nikaido's lab coat. Kujo looked on, trying to keep from laughing.

"Dr. Kujo, when do you think you can come to tutor me next?" Maki asked.

"How's tomorrow night?"

"Great. I'm going to feed the animals now." With her father's coat in her arms, she left.

Nikaido sighed as he watched his daughter go. "She's more and more like her mother every day. She must still yearn for her mother's touch, but I have to say she's coming up nicely."

"She's completely turned into your wife. She's quite a girl—she's got the world's preeminent professor of immunology completely under her thumb."

†

When Kujo looked into the animal husbandry room, Maki was feeding the lab chimpanzee.

"Eat up now," Maki told the monkey. Though her voice was cheerful, her cheeks were wet with tears. The animals in the room were to be subjects in lab experiments the next day. Maki hastily wiped away her tears upon seeing Kujo. "I know I'm not supposed to get attached to them…"

Ignorant of its own fate, the chimpanzee inside the cage was also attached to Maki. The chimp bared its teeth defensively when Kujo bent down next to Maki.

"We're allowed to go on living happy, healthy lives because tens of thousands of animals like this chimp sacrifice their lives. But all people do is kill and hate and do whatever they please. I guess they forgot that nature is what keeps us all alive," Maki said.

Kujo peered into the girl's face. "Maki, do you think the people of this world deserve to live at the expense of sacrificing the lives of these animals?"

Maki looked at the animals and pondered the question a bit. "I don't know. But if these animals have to be sacrificed so we can live, I think we have to live the life they gave us to our fullest." Maki turned her innocent eyes on Kujo without hesitation. "Why do you ask, Dr. Kujo?"

Kujo smiled sadly and put an arm around the girl's shoulders. "I think if everyone thought the way you do, this world might change for the better." Kujo's face, which Maki could not see in the dark of the room, was twisted in anguish.

册 18-3 **Plan**

An elderly man, one Dr. Kagami, peered out the window of his office. The Shuto Expressway ran just outside the window. Behind the seemingly endless string of cars stood a mass of synthetic high rises, and in the background, a smog-filled sky peeked out timidly from behind the buildings that mostly obstructed it.

Dr. Kagami stared at the scene and muttered to no one in particular, "Is this really human progress? Even while people are aware of the bleak future from the coming food crisis, the rise in sea levels due to global warming, and the depletion of oil resources, they continue to put off making a decision. This is neither progress nor prosperity. Indeed, mankind is regressing."

Kagami let out an indignant sigh and turned toward the room. "Humans have forgotten that they are part of the earth's environment. The perfect cycle of nature exists now only in this miniature garden."

He directed a loving gaze toward the glass encasement he called a miniature garden. It was an enormous biotope enshrined in the center of the room. Inside the office of the NPO Blue Ship, at a desk tucked timidly out of the way of the biotope occupying half the room, about ten members of the organization were preparing educational leaflets about environmental issues.

An elderly man poked his head out from a private office.

"Dr. Kagami, we just received word. It's finished."

Kagami smiled at the news.

"Good, good. Well then, Matoba?"

There was a calm smile on Matoba's face.

"Yes, we'll move ahead with our plan tomorrow night."

The members looked up. Their work was over now.

"Ladies and gentlemen." Matoba took a step forward before the members. The same calm smile. It was an unshakeable look that,

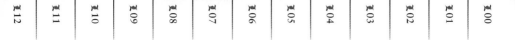

while calm, could never be taken for being kindly. The calm eyes that ruffled at nothing and the large burn mark on his cheek left a particularly strong impression on those who met the man.

Matoba spoke. "The time has come for all of us who have joined the cause in support of the ideals outlined in Dr. Kagami's great work, *Alert Status Red: The Human Species*, to take that first step toward restoring the ideal world, the society we all envision. This may be a difficult decision for all of you who have gathered for a common cause. However, at this critical turning point in human history, it is important to be prepared for a certain amount of sacrifice and imperative that a select few lead the masses. You are all chosen members of the cause. You will change the world."

Matoba had said these words countless times since he joined Blue Ship two years ago. Words designed to engrain within Kagami's followers the idea that the choice had been theirs and not one forced upon them. That only an enlightened few could choose such lofty ideals. Although such a repeated speech, short on details but long on compliments, was a very rudimentary form of manipulation, the members applauded fervently. "The day is at hand when the natural balance contained inside this garden will be restored to this world."

Kagami narrowed his eyes as if he were seeing the future encased in this miniature garden. The biotope, as its size attested, was a symbol of the hard work of the members as well as a space physically encapsulating their ideals. Inside this balanced ecosystem, every organism carried out its role as an integral part of the world.

†

Upon returning to his office, Matoba locked the door and picked up the phone.

His English was fluent. Laughing intermittently, he proceeded with the negotiation.

"Now, now, I believe you're taking advantage of me. You would be acquiring a revolutionary deterrent, one able to replace the nuclear weapon. I would think four billion dollars is a bargain."

Alone now, Matoba's smile had changed into a cynical sneer. The smile looked even more twisted by the scar on his cheek, but no one was present to witness the transformation.

"You drive a hard bargain, General. Perhaps you would have made a better businessman than a military man."

Matoba spun the globe on his meticulously organized desk, as though he already ruled it.

"I see. So you want to see its effects first."

Ⅼ17-1　Break-In

System Intruder Alert
　　...July 13, 02:32:53...
　　...Number of servers routed, 5...
　　...Firewalls breached 3/5...
　　...Recovering log → Tracking OK...
　　...Intruder identified

　　Professor Nikaido let out a quiet sigh as he ran the security check. The hacking defense system, developed by Wammy's House's Q and given to him by his personal friend Watari, had identified the perpetrator who had cleverly routed through several servers all over the world on its way into the lab's system.

　　"Accessed from inside the lab..."

　　Unwilling to accept the truth, Nikaido silently ran the security check again and again. He stared at the same result displayed on the monitor and sighed deeply.

　　It was just past eleven p.m. and there was no one else in the lab. Nikaido's eyes wandered in search of something. *Just as I'm unable to see a virus without a microscope, it seems I haven't been able to see people for who they are.* A disgusted smile escaped his lips. He stared at the teacup in his hand but did not drink the tea that Kujo had made for

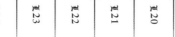

him, which was now cold.

Suddenly an alarm went off. The surveillance monitor showed an image of a group of men, masked and armed with rifles, attempting to break into the lab. Switching to a different camera, Nikaido found the guard in the security room slumped over unconscious. He appeared to have been drugged.

Quietly Nikaido closed his eyes.

For as long as he'd been handling the virus, which had the potential to become a more powerful weapon than even nuclear warheads, he had been preparing for exactly this situation. He turned to the computer and began to type furiously. After sending one email, he deleted all his files using the emergency system created by Q.

The intruders walked calmly into the lab only a second later.

"Professor Nikaido, you must be very busy, but we'd like a moment of your time." The masked man appearing to be the leader of the group announced their arrival in a polite manner belied by his threatening appearance.

"I don't believe you have an appointment," Nikaido said.

"We won't take too much of your time. We'll be on our way as soon as we accomplish what we came here for."

"And what might that be?"

The leader sat down on the sofa, and the man standing next to him answered in his stead. "We shouldn't have to tell you, now should we?" He held up his rifle.

"If I value my life… Is that it? I deal with deadly viruses every day. I'm not afraid to die."

A woman in a miniskirt came forward. "Aww, that's what I thought you'd say. Which is why we invited a special guest!" she said, snapping her fingers excitedly in a way that seemed entirely inappropriate for the situation.

"No!" Nikaido's face grew pale as he stood up.

"No! Let go…let me go!" Maki struggled to break free as she was brought before the man relaxing on the sofa.

"She must have come to check on why you're so late coming home. Saved us the trouble!"

"I'd rather not do anything extreme, so I wish you'd quietly do as we ask. As you can see," the group's leader shrugged, glancing behind him, "they're rather hot-tempered."

The younger members standing behind him snickered.

Nikaido glared at the man on the sofa. "So you're here for the virus. I can only imagine the foolish scheme you'd hatch if I were to hand over the virus to the likes of someone who'd resort to this to get what they wanted."

"Foolish, you say?" the man repeated, standing up slowly. With that ever-present smile peeking out from behind the mask, he grabbed Nikaido by the collar and kneed him in the pit of the stomach.

Nikaido staggered back coughing and fell into a chair.

"Not nearly as foolish as you, who would create a weapon such as the virus, knowing that the Japanese government and the U.S. would have their way with it."

"You're wrong! My father wouldn't make a weapon. Liar! Let me go!" Maki, whose arms were being held behind her, tried to writhe free.

"Oh, shut your yap, will you? I hate the sound of kids' voices. Now I'm getting annoyed." The young woman began to fiddle with the stiletto knife hanging at her waist. The blade glimmered.

Nikaido bit his lip and growled, "The virus and antidote are being stored in deep-freeze containers in separate compartments. They can only be opened with my password and biometric authentication."

"Then if you'll please show us the way."

"Daddy, don't give it to them!" Maki shouted as Nikaido was marched toward the storage compartments with a rifle in his back. He choked out, "I only completed the antidote last night. I haven't reported it to anyone yet. Just how did the information get leaked?"

The leader laughed. "Well now, are you saying that a preeminent virologist such as yourself isn't able to identify the source of the virus?" They arrived at the storage compartment, and Nikaido had no choice but to hand the ampule of the virus to the group's leader. Then on to the next storage compartment. Nikaido took the ampule of the antidote in his hand and stopped.

The world will end if they use this. Nikaido hesitated and asked, "What will you use it for?"

"Not to worry. We will use it to achieve world peace," said the group's leader.

Nikaido fixed his eyes on the man and said, "The world peace you speak of is one that's only convenient to you. You're the same as that Kira, who went around killing criminals without regard for the law."

The leader in the mask appeared unruffled. "The same as Kira— for us, that would be a high compliment. Our will to create an ideal society is no less passionate than that of Kira."

Nikaido closed his eyes upon hearing the words. When he opened them again, there was a quiet determination in his eyes. Maki swallowed hard. "Don't lose sight of what you have to do. Until the very last moment..." muttered Nikaido to himself, as if to make certain of his own resolve. In the next instant, he smashed the ampule on the floor and threw himself at one of the men holding a rifle.

The man's fingers inadvertently pulled the trigger. The rifle crack rang throughout the room and everything stopped.

"I...I shot him," the man said, visibly upset even with his face masked. "It wasn't my fault." He looked down at Nikaido. The scientist had sunk to his knees; the bullet had opened up his chest.

"Y-you came at me first," the man said. He dropped the rifle with a bewildered look. Evidently he had never shot anyone before now.

Gasping for air, Nikaido choked out, "I deleted...the antidote...

data... If I die...you won't be able to...produce it." Slowly, Nikaido fell forward and collapsed.

"Daddy!" Maki, who had stood helplessly by, shook off the arms holding her and made a run for it.

"Hey, stop!"

Maki slipped through the arms trying to grab her, dropped down and crawled between one man's legs. The men reached to grab her, but their long rifles got in the way, clanging against one another.She bolted out of the storage room, shutting the door behind her, and wedged the handle end of a mop against the door.

"Break it down!"

The men quickly broke down the door, but Maki was already gone.

"The stairs! She went up!"

"We put guards on all the exits. She won't get away!"

The men hit the steps and ran immediately into a stream of blinding fire retardant. Maki filled the narrow corridor with the foam from the top of the steps, then flung the empty canister at the nearest target.

"Argh!"

More fire extinguishers—three of them this time—took a good bounce off the edge of the stairs and slammed into legs and arms and even a masked forehead.

By the time the exhaust settled onto the slick steps, the girl was gone again.

"Check the rooms!"

"Got it."

The men were angry now and kicked open doors with what might be called glee.

"I heard something in here!"

"Open it!"

Kicking down the door, the men burst into the room without

bothering to check the sign on it. Instantly they fell over backward as a monkey flew right at them.

"Dammit, now you're gonna get it!" shouted the red-faced man, who threw off his mask after being scratched up and down by the monkey.

Meanwhile, Maki took refuge inside her father's office. She saw the lab coat hanging on the wall and was reminded of the image of her father's dying moments. She could no longer stifle the sobs. Touching the coat gently, she remembered what her father had told her: *Maki, if something happens to me, grab what's in the safe and run. You have to save the world.*

Replaying her father's instructions inside her head, Maki entered a number on the touchpad and opened the safe.

"Daddy...what is this?"

Inside the safe was a teddy bear.

For a moment she stared at it blankly, but the menacing footsteps drew closer and closer by the second. She nodded resolutely, stepped inside the safe, and closed the door from inside. Just as the door clacked shut, the men arrived out of breath. They looked at each other and laughed.

"Just like a child. What is she going to do locked up inside the safe?"

The leader, finally strolling in, said, "Like a mouse in a trap. We should be able to find out the access code to the safe easily enough." Then he ordered, "Get it open, Yoshizawa. Quickly."

"Yes, sir."

With a laptop and two alligator clips, the man called Yoshizawa went to work, hacking the lock and its programming simultaneously. It took only a few minutes. He pulled opened the safe door and peered inside.

"Come on out. Wait until I get my hands on you," he said with an air of bravado, though he had already taken both a fire extinguisher and a monkey to the face. Cautiously he set foot inside the safe one step at a time. However, he returned immediately with a dismayed look. "Mr. Matoba, there's a trap door."

Matoba, the leader, put a hand to his head and looked up at the ceiling dramatically. "We've been had. She must have gone into the underground corridors."

"Should we go after her?"

"Don't bother, Konishi," replied Matoba. He took off his mask and sat on the sofa. "The professor said he destroyed all the data on the virus."

"Uh, yes…" said Konishi, who'd been checking the data on the professor's computer. With his eyes blinking timidly from behind his glasses, Konishi shook his head. "Everything's been deleted. The data can't be recovered."

Unruffled, Matoba muttered, "As long as he was aware of the possibility that the virus could be used by terrorists, he would never dispose of the research results completely. The data must be somewhere else. To whom would he entrust it?"

"Someone he trusts the most…his daughter?" offered Yoshizawa.

Matoba nodded. "He sacrificed himself to secure her escape. There's no telling who the girl might have helping her. We will have to take a more indirect approach. But the first step is to find the girl."

Though inwardly he cursed the men's failure, Matoba did not let on. He was already planning their next move.

"But Mr. Matoba, we now have the virus. Couldn't we carry out the plan with the virus alone?"

Matoba glared at Yoshizawa. "Listen to yourself! If we do that, you and the other people who are indispensable to the new world are liable to become victims. I won't jeopardize the people who support our plan!"

"Mr. Matoba—"

"Yoshizawa, you must not degrade what we are trying to accomplish to an act of terrorism. I will not allow anyone to disgrace this

plan that is to be carried out for a noble cause."

Since Matoba was rarely one to raise his voice, his concern for the members had the effect of boosting morale. To Matoba, the members of the organization were nothing more than pawns to be used. For these pawns to perform effectively, however, they could not yet know their real purpose.

"Oh, Mr. Matoba! What do you want me to do with the body? By morning, the other researchers will be back." Hatsune listlessly took off her mask. Tracing the blade of her stiletto knife with her finger, she seemed dissatisfied to have done so little.

"Fortunately, this is a level four experimental facility," Matoba said matter-of-factly, sitting in Nikaido's chair. "No one will discover the body if we incinerate it along with the infected lab animals. We'll make it look like Professor Nikaido went on a little trip."

L 17-2 Job

There were two piles on the table in front of L. One was a sweets tower of *dango, youkan, manju,* and candies stacked to L's aesthetic taste. Panda-shaped cookies from a box of Panda's March marched in a line atop the tower.

The other was a pile of cell phones. Scrawled on the backs of each were the names of heads of state, directors of intelligence agencies, as well as the names of religious leaders, CEOs of global corporations, and mob bosses, all of whom essentially had a hand in running the world. These phones were L's personal hotlines.

"See the man leaving the church?" L said, looking up at the monitor. "He's the serial killer murdering the clergymen. The probability is 86 percent. If he's the culprit, we'll find mementos of each of his victims in the crypt under the church."

"Concerning the DSGE's request to investigate the death of Princess Joanne, I have evidence to prove the boating accident was an assassination," he said into another phone.

"I discovered a hidden account in the Cayman Islands. Look at the deposit records and the amount of the ransom. The dates, times, and amounts match up. The account belongs to—"

As he picked up yet another new cell phone between his fingers, L spoke fluently in Italian, French, and English, working to resolve the unsolved cases compiled by Watari.

Every so often, L's hand reached instead for the sweets tower, and the smiling panda-shaped cookies made one final march before disappearing into L's mouth. With each case solved, L tossed the case file along with a cell phone in a trash bin marked DONE.

"You're throwing those away?" asked Suruga. He was wearing an apron. Suruga had become a housekeeper of sorts since arriving at the Kira Investigation building and was cleaning L's suite.

"I won't be needing them anymore. Another L will take over in my place."

Suruga went back to being an agent for a moment and stared at L's curved back. Two days had passed since he infiltrated the Kira Investigation Headquarters. No one else had come or gone, and while this man appeared to be L, his occasional reference to "another L" bothered Suruga. Surely he didn't seem to be in contact with anyone else. A bluff? Or…Suruga crossed his arms and sighed, the truth eluding him.

Soon the piles of snacks and cell phones were gone. Only the cell phone marked "President of the United States" was spared the trash bin and stuffed in L's pocket.

L looked up mechanically. His face looked lost and unfocussed. L seemed put at a loss by the first free moment he'd had since the world had recognized him as a peerless and unrivaled detective.

L pressed a thumb to his mouth, like a child who lost his way, and stared down at his wristwatch. A watch with its glass face cracked and the time stopped at 7:05. A chime signaled the arrival of a new message. L turned to the computer —a calligraphic W was displayed on the screen. It was an email from Professor Nikaido.

Watari, take care of my daughter—

L stared at the short message for a moment. Then he glanced at the picture of Watari on the desk. "Is this to be my last job, Watari?"

Like a zombie out of an old horror movie, he thrust out both arms and left his fingers dangling. He walked across the room to another table with another pile, this one of open and idle laptop computers. Moving just his fingers, L operated several computers simultaneously. Professor Nikaido's past achievements, recent activities, conference papers. A torrent of words rained down each of the screens, which L took in all at once. Then he got to work accessing the internal networks of the world's intelligence agencies. Using multiple servers as springboards, he exploited a vulnerability to enter each system, used a dummy password, counteracted a hacker trap with a mirror trap, and masked the source while eliminating any trace of unauthorized activity.

Biting his fingernails, L read every file marked TOP SECRET or CONFIDENTIAL.

"A new type of Ebola-like hemorrhagic fever in interior Congo… antidote being developed…level four research facility in Japan…"

From the information culled from multiple sources, L was able to determine Nikaido's current situation, the power of the enemy forces, and the likelihood that Nikaido was in trouble, and calculated the overall rate of danger.

"Eighty-three percent probability…"

His nail biting grew louder, actually echoing across the room. Suruga turned around, frightened by the noise, but with his pale face tinted red by the blinking lights on the screen, L continued to bite his nails as if the vibrations sent to his head helped him to think.

A warning alarm suddenly went off, and a shadow appeared on the camera monitoring the entrance. A girl holding a teddy bear stood at the door.

Maki Nikaido, age 10; nationality: Japanese; sex: female; daughter of Kimihiko Nikaido, distinguished professor at Wammy's House.

The information came up instantly on the facial recognition system. She was the same girl L had encountered in Los Angeles. Evidently Watari had investigated her afterwards and uploaded the information into the system.

L deactivated the system and allowed the girl inside. As soon as he looked at her, L went straight to the point without bothering to ask who she was. "Watari isn't here. Has something happened to your father?"

Maki gave a startled look and began to cry where she stood.

"Hey, what's going on here?" Suruga ran to her side.

"It must have been hard. You were smart to come here," L said, ascertaining that his 83 percent probability had been on the mark. He bent down in front of the girl and offered her a special dango made from skewering five manju on a stick. "Sweets can help calm the nerves."

Maki held tight to her teddy bear and shook her head. It took several moments for her to calm down.

"I suppose no one would suspect the safe would lead to a secret passage. So Professor Nikaido instructed you to take what was inside and run if anything happened to him. What is it that you took from the safe?" L asked.

Maki warily hid the teddy bear, her only possession, behind her back. "My father said to ask for a Mr. Watari's help. If you're not him, I can't trust you 100 percent just yet."

Far from getting angry at the girl who glared at him, L nodded in approval and said, "A correct response. If you have something to protect, you should only give it to someone you trust. The way your father entrusted it to you."

"So where is Mr. Watari?"

"Watari isn't here."

"When will he be back?"

"He isn't coming back."

Maki looked to Suruga for help.

Sensing L's reluctance to reveal the truth himself, Suruga answered instead. "Maki, Watari suffered the same fate as your father. He was killed by some bad people."

"What...?" Maki couldn't help but stare at L, who jumped onto the sofa and turned his back, biting his nails.

"I am the one who killed Watari. If I hadn't failed, he would still..." L's slouch grew rounder as he sat on the sofa with his knees tucked tightly against his chest. He looked like a child who didn't know what to do with arms and legs that had grown too long. To Maki, he seemed to be burdened by the weight of something very heavy that she could not see.

L 16   Kujo

The next afternoon, the security system picked up the presence of a petite woman at the entrance.

"Oh, it's Dr. Kujo!" said Maki, scampering to the monitor.

"Who's that?" asked L. He did not take his eyes off the monitor, as he drowned the bean dessert from Asakusa's Umemura in black syrup.

"She works at my father's research lab. She also tutors me and helps with my homework. Let her in."

"Hello? She's a beauty, isn't she? Though not so much beautiful as pretty…" Suruga said, leaning forward at the sight of the woman in the monitor.

"Hey, don't try anything funny! Dr. Kujo is very shy, so you'll scare her. Besides, she's probably older than you," Maki said.

"Really? Over thirty? Sure doesn't look it."

For a moment L observed Kujo looking troubled by the strict security, then turned on the microphone.

"Dr. Kujo, the security system is turned on. I am going to activate the voice guidance program. Please follow the instructions to undergo the fingerprint and retinal scans, and the metal detector scan. Your belongings will also be subjected to scans by X-ray."

Kujo gave a slight nod in the monitor.

This is a change from when I first got here. Even though Suruga felt

discomfited by the strict security check imposed on Kujo as compared to his own entrance, he convinced himself that the change in procedure might be attributed to his successful infiltration.

"Dr. Kujo!" Maki ran to her when she entered the room.

"Maki, I'm so glad you're safe."

With the tension drained out of her upon seeing a familiar face, Maki broke down sobbing in Kujo's arms. Kujo stroked the girl's head again and again.

The doctor bowed toward L and Suruga and said, "Thank you for looking after Maki. My name is Kujo. I'm an assistant at Professor Nikaido's laboratory. The professor and Maki have been very kind and treated me like family."

"Pleased to meet you, Dr. Kujo, I'm Ryuzaki. How did you find this place?" L introduced himself perfunctorily, in a monotone, as if ignoring her polite introduction.

Kujo's face grew clouded by the questioning tone. "Ah...I found Professor Nikaido's cell phone in the lab. His phone acts as a GPS device for Maki's cell phone—"

"A child abduction prevention device. Understandable considering the professor's research dealt with dangerous viruses. There's no telling when the family could be in danger." Suruga cut in on the conversation and held out a hand. "The name's Suruga, FBI Los Angeles Bureau. A pleasure to meet you."

Kujo's delicate hand fit neatly inside Suruga's. Despite being troubled by Suruga's grip on her hand, she asked timidly, "Um... excuse me, Mr. Suruga. What is FBI?"

"Huh? You don't know the FBI. Oh..." Suruga deflated visibly.

"Even I know who the FBI are, Dr. Kujo. They're in all the American spy movies," Maki said with a giggle.

Kujo blushed and bowed repeatedly toward Suruga. "I'm sorry. I'm afraid I don't know much." Then she turned to the child. "Maki, where is the professor?"

Maki fell silent, her cheerful mood now gone. L informed Kujo of Professor Nikaido's murder and how Maki had managed to escape and come here.

"No! Is it true?" Kujo's face became ashen as she shook her head. She looked at the girl's downcast face and held her tightly. "Maki, how difficult this must have been for you. You were very brave." Tears rolled down Kujo's face as she patted the child's back. A sympathetic Suruga hastily turned his back and sniffled. But when he saw L observing the two of them soberly, as if such emotions were alien to him, Suruga felt embarrassed. *I guess he isn't known as a kinky bizarre murder-loving detective who never gets involved unless there are more than ten bodies for nothing.* Suruga recalled the FBI's profile on L and was oddly impressed.

Wiping away her tears, Kujo faced L and asked, "Mr. Ryuzaki. I realize this may be an imposition, but would it be possible for me to stay here with Maki just until I can be sure that she's no longer in danger? Now that the professor is gone, I have to be the one to protect her." Though she seemed reserved, there was a steeliness in her eyes of someone who had something precious to protect.

"That would be fine. This building has room enough to accommodate over twenty guests. Please use any room you like," L said. "But so long as we have yet to learn who is after Maki, she will not leave this building. And you will refrain from going out as much as possible."

"I understand."

"Dr. Kujo, take the room next to mine. Come on, I'll show you!"

After Maki led Kujo by the arm out of the room, Suruga whispered in L's ear, "Hey, Ryuzaki. She's a little naïve, but beautiful. Things are going to be more exciting around here, eh?"

L looked lost, as if he'd been asked his opinion about some profound impressionist painting. "Beautiful...? Such things, I don't know about."

†

After dinner Maki went into Kujo's room and was telling the doctor everything that had happened since yesterday. L was playing himself in chess as usual, with a *Rikishi monaka* from Ryogoku sticking out of his mouth. Suruga, alone and with nothing to do, wandered over to the sofa.

"Ryuzaki, how much fun is it playing alone? I can play you, if you'd like. I'm pretty—" Suruga stopped mid-sentence. L was moving the pieces differently than by the established rules. "Hey, Ryuzaki. Maybe you've got the game mixed up with *shogi* because you're in Japan. You're not allowed to use the pieces you captured as your own in chess."

Turning a deaf ear, L moved a knight to and fro in enemy territory. Suruga peered over from behind the sofa and realized L wasn't looking at the chessboard at all. He followed L's gaze to a monitor hidden by his feet. Pictured onscreen was surveillance video of Kujo's room. He had been watching Kujo talking to Maki.

"You pretended not to be interested, but you've been checking her out on the surveillance camera. You perverted—"

"I—" the sandwich fell from his mouth— "don't believe Dr. Kujo has come here with the purpose of protecting Maki, but for another purpose," L interrupted.

"You don't think she's involved with the group that attacked Maki and Professor Nikaido, do you? That's impossible." Suruga shook his head, recalling Kujo's naïve manner.

"While she may have appeared to look uncomfortable when she first arrived here, she was alert and checking the security cameras. I am going to keep her under twenty-four-hour surveillance. Please don't tell Dr. Kujo or Maki about this."

†

"Sixty-six seconds to the second floor. Wait six seconds and move to north end of hall. Seventy-five seconds, take cover in fuel storage room. Eighty-one seconds, back out to the hall. Eighty-seven seconds, deactivate lock. Ninety seconds, arrive at destination."

Suruga repeated several dance-like steps while staring down at the stopwatch setting on his watch, then slipped into the server room.

The Kira Investigation Headquarters was monitored via surveillance cameras placed all throughout the building. At the moment, L was monitoring ninety locations on three monitors, which were on a ninety second loop that switched to a different camera every three seconds.

After Suruga had figured out the sequential pattern, it had become his late-night routine to sneak into the server room without being detected. In this room alone there were no surveillance cameras. Inside the room were the rows of servers that controlled the Kira Investigation Headquarters. They buzzed quietly, unaware that their primary goal of tracking Kira was finished.

"Man, is the AC cold in here. I guess the only things in here are computers anyway."

Suruga took out his cell phone to check in with the Bureau, but it was at this moment he finally realized he was not alone.

"Good evening, Mr. Suruga."

Kujo smiled at Suruga and turned her attention back to a laptop, without even a hint of shock or guilt over having been found acting in secret.

"What are you doing here, Kujo?"

"I'm trying to break into the system, but it's so heavily blocked that this laptop won't do. I'll need a supercomputer to find a way in. If it was impossible to hack into the system from the outside, I was

hoping maybe from the inside..." Her demure tone and smile had not changed, which seemed to exaggerate her sudden change all the more.

"So you didn't come here just to protect the girl after all." Suruga drew closer, still unsure of her intentions.

"And you? What business do you have in this camera-free room?" she asked, pointing out his own culpability, to which Suruga nodded in acknowledgement.

"Ryuzaki suspects something's up. He's been monitoring your room."

"I expected as much. The man known as the world's top detective wouldn't be so careless."

Suruga was sure of it now. Kujo was aware of Ryuzaki's identity as well as the purpose behind the building's advanced equipment and security. There was a hint of defiance behind Kujo's eyes.

"Who the hell are you?" Suruga asked. "Are you with the group who's after Maki?"

Taking her fingers off the keyboard, Kujo looked up thoughtfully. "Not even Maki knows this." Slowly she spun the chair around to face Suruga and continued, "I'm an undercover agent with the Tokyo Police Department, Public Security Bureau, Third Foreign Affairs Division."

"Third Foreign Affairs Division—you mean the counterterrorism division?"

Kujo nodded, at which point Suruga took a moment to study her. The delicately built woman before him and a word as frightening as *counterterrorism* just did not compute inside Suruga's head. The smile on her prim lips became faintly seductive as she gauged the rate of his comprehension.

Damn, women are scary, Suruga thought, thinking too of Naomi for some reason. Then he felt somewhat peeved that L, who was clearly inexperienced with women, had been better at reading Kujo.

"So your not knowing about the FBI was just an act."

The mischievous smile on her face was answer enough. How could anyone with the police department not know the FBI? "What is that you're after?"

"After we received information that Professor Nikaido had smuggled a deadly virus into Japan, I was sent to infiltrate his lab posing as a research assistant," she explained without hesitation. "We picked up activity of several terrorist groups who were after the virus, and we believe one of them is responsible for the professor's murder. Since all of the data on the virus and its antidote is missing, I figured the professor might have given it to Maki. As you know, a virus can be mass-produced relatively cheaply and can be carried around in a pocket—a perfect weapon for terrorist organizations. But if there's one flaw in using a virus weapon, it would have to be the 'boomerang' effect—if you were to use the virus in an attack, it might spread and come back to infect you."

"But if you had an effective antidote, that flaw could be neutralized. And an ultimate weapon is born."

"Yes, if both the virus and the antidote were to fall into the hands of a terrorist group, the world could be at an end."

"So your aim is to secure the antidote data that Professor Nikaido entrusted to his daughter."

Kujo nodded. "Fortunately, Maki trusts me. But if she were to find out that I'm with the police who'd been sent to infiltrate her father's lab, I don't know what she might do. Not to mention, I've encountered a new problem since coming here."

"A new problem?"

She stared at him as if he should know the answer.

So that's it, Suruga thought. The police department had sent an undercover agent based on the same fears held by the FBI.

"L."

"Yes. Of course, it's my job to prevent the antidote data from

falling into the hands of terrorists. But even more than that, we're afraid of L's coming into possession of the data. It would be helpful just to know whether Maki still has the data or if he is already in possession of it. But since he's been listening in on my conversations with Maki...If he would at least eat the meals that I make, I could slip him a pill and do some investigating, but he didn't even touch dinner."

Kujo let out at sigh and stretched a bit in her seat with both fists clenched next to her ears. Such childish mannerisms seemed incongruous with her mature countenance, yet they captivated Suruga.

She noticed his eyes on her and stood up hastily, blushing. "Well, I should be getting back now. I'm supposed to be taking a bath." Tucking the laptop under her arm, she, like Suruga, set her watch in stopwatch mode in preparation for the way back. As she passed Suruga on the way out, she stopped as if she'd suddenly remembered something.

"By the way Mr. Suruga, what is it that you're after?"

"The instrument Kira was using to murder his victims. We can't allow the killing weapon to remain in L's possession."

"Then what would you say to a partnership?"

"A partnership? How do you mean?"

She smiled suggestively as her lithe fingers brushed against his arm. "You need Kira's instrument of death and I need the antidote data. Our roles and what we are after may be different, but our goal is essentially the same. Wouldn't it be wise to work together?"

𝕷 15   Agreement

There had been an awkward tension between Suruga and Kujo since morning. Every time Suruga spoke to her, Kujo answered only perfunctorily and appeared to be avoiding him. Observing them from the sofa, L enjoyed his extra-sweet morning coffee from a bowl-sized cup, which he held in both hands like an offering.

"It seems you've fallen out of favor with Dr. Kujo," L pointed out as soon as Kujo disappeared into the kitchen with the dishes.

"Yeah, well…you know," Suruga replied.

"Hey, you didn't try anything funny with Dr. Kujo, did you?" Maki asked. Suruga shrank his large frame apologetically.

"I-I tried to sweet-talk her, you know, out of habit from my days living in the States, and she completely shot me down."

"See? I told you not to try anything!" Maki ran into the kitchen to check on Kujo. Suruga scratched his head awkwardly.

"Perhaps this isn't for me to say, but it's inappropriate to go to a lady's room at that hour."

"So you think so too—hey, wait! You weren't…" Rushing to the sofa, Suruga pushed L aside and looked into the monitor hidden by his feet. As expected, the monitor showed the image of Kujo washing dishes in the kitchen. "You weren't watching when I was in Kujo's room last night were you?"

"Of course."

"Damn, that's what I was afraid of! You pervert!"

"There's no need to be embarrassed, Mr. Suruga."

"It's not that I'm embarrassed…"

"Why are you being so serious, Mr. Suruga?" L asked, his face sober.

Suruga walked away with no answer but a blush. It had been worth the trouble to put on a show if L had been watching. After all, the quarrel enacted inside Kujo's room had all been for L's benefit.

†

"I wonder if we can plant a bug in the Operations Room. It would help if we could listen in on L's conversations with Maki when we're not there."

"You might be able to smuggle it onto the premises, Mr. Suruga, but L is sure to find it if we plant it in the Operations Room. That room likely has an alarm that reacts to any signal a bug would transmit," Kujo said. She was wearing a summery sleeveless dress today. The air conditioner inside the server room was set at a lower temperature than the rest of the rooms, and perhaps due to the cold, Kujo occasionally wrapped her arms around her shoulders. Suruga couldn't help but admire how white her exposed arms were.

"Is something the matter?" she asked.

"Um…you must be cold." Suruga took off his jacket and draped it around her shoulders. After hesitating a bit, Kujo thanked him with a shy smile. Suruga was aware that he was beginning to have feelings that were something more than camaradarie between fellow operatives.

"Mr. Suruga, would you happen to have more than one cell phone?"

"Sure I do." Due to the nature of his job, he often kept two cell phones, which he used for different purposes.

"Then we'll be able to use these as listening devices."

†

That night Suruga made up an excuse of not feeing well and retired to his room early. Though he knew he wasn't being watched, he jumped into bed and slipped under the covers first before taking out his cell phone. Earlier he had made a point of "forgetting" his other phone near the sofa where L usually sat. Since the phone was on auto pick-up, if he called the phone, it was possible to be connected without the phone ringing.

As he listened in, Suruga heard two voices:

"Then you were living in the same neighborhood as Misa Amane in Osaka?"

"Yes. Misa was known around the neighborhood for being pretty. We also used to go on vacation together because our families were close."

"You knew Misa Amane before she made her debut? I'm jealous."

L did sound green with envy, in contrast with his usual stoic demeanor. With Maki and her Osaka dialect and L with his strangely polite way of speaking, they continued this odd exchange like a bad comedy team. After Suruga listened for about half an hour, L finally broached the subject Suruga wanted to hear.

"You really won't give me the data no matter how much I ask?"

"Nope. I'm not handing over this data to anyone."

"Then what would you say to a trade for my cherished notebook?"

"A notebook?"

"Yes. It's more precious than my own life. Would you trade the data for that?"

"Well...all right. If you feel that strongly about it."

"Thank you. Here's my notebook."

"Ryuzaki, this is a bag of potato chips."

"Yes, the notebook is inside. Nobody would think anything impor-tant would be inside a bag of potato chips, don't you think?"

Dammit if you aren't the only one who'd hide something so important in a place like that! Suruga wanted to shout, but had to stop himself since, unlike a proper listening device, they would also hear him on the other end of the cell phone if he spoke.

"Yeah, but..." Maki said, still suspicious.

"I'll put the data you gave me in a different bag of potato chips and keep it in my snacks compartment for safekeeping. It will be a lot safer than putting it in a normal safe."

"You won't eat it by mistake, will you, Ryuzaki?"

L answered in his oddly confident way, "Don't worry. I don't eat consommé-flavor."

L14 Strategy

For Suruga, whose specialty was covert investigation, getting the bags of potato chips without being seen by L, Maki, or the surveillance cameras was simple. "Shall we begin our regular strategy meeting?" quipped Suruga in the server room. His arms were full.

"Tonight we even have a lovely dessert," Kujo replied. "You didn't open them?"

"I figured we'd share that pleasure together." Suruga opened the bag containing the data first. A capsule with a microchip inside rolled out from among the potato chips. "Bingo!"

Kujo took the microchip and got to work on the laptop. However, her finger on the mouse button stopped clicking almost immediately. "These are…graphic files."

"What is this?"

"These look like Maki's family pictures. She's still young here, so they must be from a couple years ago."

The pictures were of a family vacation the Nikaidos had taken with the Amane family when they lived in Osaka. Among them were pictures of Misa Amane before her modeling debut, which were of supreme importance to L, but of course, Suruga and Kujo had no way of knowing that. They looked at each other with a feeling of foreboding.

"What about the notebook?" Kujo said as she opened the other bag. In it was a black college-ruled notebook wrapped inside a plastic bag. "Is this what Kira was using to murder his victims?"

"Yes, the Death Note. According to L's report, you can kill a person just by writing their name in this notebook."

The two were tense in the presence of the ultimate killing weapon. Slowly Suruga turned the page. The pages were practically blackened with words. "...Funawa's *imo youkan*...*kusa dango* from Shibamata, *Rikishi monaka* from Ryogoku, *mamekan* from Asakusa, *Kototoi dango* from Mukoujima, Toraya's *youkan*...what the hell?"

"They're all famous sweets from around Tokyo."

They were rendered speechless by the unexpected contents of the notebook.

It was a list of sweets L had sampled since coming to Japan with each of the items ranked in L's own discriminating, opinionated style. While it might have been more precious to L than his own life, to Suruga and Kujo the notebook was worthless.

"Do you mean to tell me that L saw this coming?" Suruga threw the notebook aside and held his head in his hands. With her arms folded across her chest, Kujo pressed her right hand against her temple.

"I figured the probability of L producing the real things was only about 3 percent anyway."

Though Suruga thought she sounded a lot like L just then, that she didn't seem terribly disappointed was surprising. "You have something else in mind?"

"Yes, but it could get complicated. It could also get dangerous, for you too, but if we don't risk it, L might never bring the real notebook or antidote data out in the open."

Suruga thought about it as he ran a hand over his growing stubble. It seemed evident that nothing more would come from continuing the investigation as he had. And besides, the Bureau was anxious to

hear some good news. "What's your strategy?" he asked.

"Fortunately, Maki trusts me, and L will also do what she says. We'll use that to set a trap." Kujo's eyes glowed with the determination to match wits with the world's greatest detective. "I'm going to make him write my name in the Death Note."

𝕃 13-1 Hostage

"Ryuzaki, we've got an alert! Three suspicious cars surrounding the building." Suruga threw off his apron, having returned from grocery shopping, and suddenly he was an FBI agent again.

L, who was hard at work building a tower out of thinly cut slices of Toraya's youkan, tapped on the laptop to bring up a picture of the entrance on the monitor. Though the men who got out of the cars looked like businessmen in suits, it was clear from their awkward movements that they were concealing weapons.

"It's all right," L said. "The security here is impenetrable." L resumed building his tower without any sign of panic. However, the intruders produced an electronic device to break into the entry system and began to disable the security levels one by one. The system-error warning rang throughout the building.

So far, so good. Suruga cautiously watched L's movements while looking panicked on the surface.

The first stage of Kujo's strategy was to break into the Kira Investigation Headquarters by crashing the security system, forcing L to flee the building. In an emergency, he was sure to take the Death Note and antidote data with him. Suruga, who unlike Kujo could go in and out of the building without a security check, had smuggled in the necessary equipment and set it up. By attacking the system simultaneously from inside and out, they were able to disable the security. Of course, Kujo had told him that the men from the counterterrorism division would be posing as the intruders.

The men busting through the entrance was the last image on the surveillance camera before it went down. The youkan tower, approaching a new height record, toppled over at the same time.

"It appears they have an expert hacker on their side. Maki, Mr. Suruga, we're leaving. There's a customized escape vehicle in the garage. Where is Dr. Kujo?" L said.

"She went home to get a change of clothes."

Hopping off the couch, L grabbed Maki with his right hand and a bag of sweets with the left and ran. But he quickly put on the brakes and rushed back to the middle of the room.

"What are you doing? Hurry!" L pressed the button hidden beneath the table and a sturdy duralumin case emerged from under the table. Weighing the value of the case and the bag of sweets as if on a scale, L gave up the bag reluctantly and ran with the duralumin case in his hands, though he did manage to stick a lollipop in his mouth as he ran.

†

"Ryuzaki, this is the Kira Investigation Headquarters. Don't you have something better than this?" It was no wonder Suruga was shocked. The vehicle that Ryuzaki hopped into was the bright green crepe truck. L frowned at the criticism.

"This happens to be a sophisticated, new mobile operations room. We will bust our way out, so hang on tight."

The crepe truck burst through the camouflaged exit. Three cars came after them at once, and in a matter of seconds, they were on their tail.

"At this speed, they're going to be on us in no time. Hey, the axle!

The brakes! Drive for godsakes!" Suruga shouted as he smacked his head repeatedly against the low ceiling of the truck.

Just as he had been on the sofa, L was perched on top of the driver's seat with his legs folded against his chest, the steering wheel pinched between the fingers of his right hand and the lollipop clutched in his left. "It's all right," he said. "The traffic conditions, the timing of the traffic lights, road regulations, and the times of train crossings have all been inputted into the computer, so this vehicle will choose our best escape route and speed."

True to L's word, despite creeping along slowly, the truck sailed past a light just before it turned to elude one car, slipped into an alley barely wide enough for the truck to pass to elude a second, and caught just the moment to blow past a slowly descending railroad crossing to shake off all three cars.

After confirming their safety in the mirror and the external camera, L slowed the truck down and tucked it out of sight in the warehouse district.

Maki turned around worriedly from the passenger seat to look at L, who was now sitting in the back of the truck. "Ryuzaki! What about Dr. Kujo? If she gets caught…"

"Surely she's smart enough to know not to go near the building if she senses something wrong." No sooner had L said it than Maki's cell phone rang. Maki's face froze upon seeing the name on the display.

"It's Dr. Kujo, isn't it?" L grabbed the phone to turn the volume up to maximum and gave it back her. Though Maki seemed none too pleased, she hit the talk button.

"Dr. Kujo! Are you okay?"

"I'm sorry, Maki…I'm afraid they got me. Can I talk to Mr. Ryu-zaki?"

L took the phone from Maki and held it pinched precariously between his fingers.

"Shall I call you Mr. Ryuzaki? I paid a visit to your home to make a proper introduction, but since you were apparently out, we'll have to do this over the phone." The voice of the man who replaced Kujo on the phone was that of a middle-aged man. Though he spoke politely, there was a note of arrogance in his voice.

"Not at all, I apologize I wasn't in when you called."

A momentary silence. It was like a wordless exchange, despite not knowing what the other looked like, to feel out the other's intentions.

"Now, I do rather appreciate people who are quick to understand. Mr. Ryuzaki, I'd like us to make a trade—the woman we have here for what the little miss has in her possession. Would you agree to such a transaction?"

"What do you intend to do with it once you have it?"

Suddenly the man's voice took on a sullen tone. "As I said, I rather prefer people who are quick to understand. Your choices are not improved by asking such a question."

"No, it's simply a matter of the potential scale of the damage. If one person's sacrifice can prevent the devastation that a killer virus might cause—"

Both Suruga and Maki turned on L before he could finish.

"Ryuzaki! What are you saying? Are you going to let Dr. Kujo just die? You can't do that!"

"Ryuzaki, right now our priority is to save Kujo!"

With the cell phone in his hand, L looked alternately at Suruga and Maki and sighed. The man on the other end stifled a laugh.

"Mr. Ryuzaki, perhaps as their leader you'd like to bring your group to a consensus."

"I understand. Where will the exchange take place?"

"Ten o'clock tonight, Yokohama. We'll be at the Yellow Box warehouse on the south edge of Daikoku Pier. I'm afraid I won't be able to offer you tea there... Ah, but it will all be over in minutes. Oh, and if you notify the police or if they should happen to find out, I'll take that to mean you've made another choice."

"I won't require any tea, but something sweet would be nice. May I speak to Dr. Kujo again?"

"Of course." The man laughed cheerfully, and in the next instant Kujo was back on the phone.

"Dr. Kujo. You managed to get caught rather easily."

"I'm sorry to trouble you," Kujo apologized weakly, but L did not let up.

"By having to rescue you, we're putting the lives of everyone at risk. You of all people should know the danger involved, having worked with Professor Nikaido."

"Ryuzaki, now isn't the time for this! We have to save her!" Maki said.

"She isn't a professional, Ryuzaki. We have no choice. I'll help. We have to save her first," Suruga said.

L let out another sigh.

†

The crepe truck was parked on a dry riverbed along the Tama River. Insect sounds filled the air, and with summer vacation approaching the sky lit up with fireworks from time to time. L sat peacefully on the roof of the crepe truck.

"I brought coffee."

A tray with two cups popped up from below. The tray of course came with a mound of sugar cubes, Suruga having come to know L's tastes over the past few days.

"Thank you. How many sugars do you take?" asked L, taking the tray from him.

"No, black's fine."

"A tired body needs sugar." Not allowing him to say otherwise, L dropped an equal number of sugar cubes in each cup. By the time

Suruga climbed up on the roof, the mound of sugar cubes was gone. Suruga cautiously took the coffee, and when he tried to stir it with a spoon, the unmelted sugar settled to the bottom and the spoon stood up on its own in the center of the cup. Bracing himself, he brought the cup to his mouth.

"This reminds me of the coffee frappé at this café I used to go to when I was undercover in Greece. The sweetness hits you right in the back of the head." He scowled after taking a sip and held his head.

"How is Maki?"

"Inside, sound asleep. She had tears on her face. Her father was murdered and now the woman she trusts was abducted. No matter how strong she may seem, it's too much for a ten-year-old girl to handle."

"You're right."

"What do you think the group's goal is anyway?" Suruga crooked his head sideways. He was well aware, of course, but for the time being, he needed to go along with the charade.

"Seeing how they carelessly allowed a child to escape, they don't appear to be a trained terrorist group. As for what they're plotting with the killer virus—"

"Either using the virus *is* the goal, or they're thinking of selling it for a profit."

"Mr. Suruga, would you do some intelligence-gathering using the FBI's network? And a background check on Dr. Kujo."

"Sure. But you still suspect Kujo after what's happened?"

L did not answer. He held the coffee cup above his head and caught the sugar dripping from the cup on his tongue.

Suruga leaned forward. "Listen, Ryuzaki. Couldn't you use the Death Note if you absolutely needed to?" he asked as if the thought had just now entered his mind.

"You're asking me—someone who's battled Kira—to use the Death Note?" L responded, his face dead serious.

With nothing more to say, Suruga rolled over on his back and looked up at the sky. "This reminds me of when I was a trainee at the academy. Naomi, Raye, and I—we used to lie on our backs exhausted after a day of training and gaze at the stars just like this."

"They wouldn't have had to die if I had been able to identify Kira sooner."

"Stop it. You risked your life to battle Kira."

L stared at Suruga as he ran a finger across the sweet residue at the bottom of the cup. "Even if the situation were to arise, the Death Note isn't effective unless we know the person's name and face. As long as we don't know the identity of the group that abducted Dr. Kujo, the Death Note is powerless."

*He didn't deny that he has the Death Note, which means...*Suruga thought, stealing a look at L's face.

Kujo was triumphantly analyzing the system in the Kira Investigation room by now, Suruga figured. Of course, L had deleted everything in the system when he fled the building, so the likelihood of finding the data she was after was slim, in which case the final stage of Kujo's strategy had to be executed.

Suruga moved to quench his thirst, remembering too late that this was no ordinary cup of coffee, and grabbed the back of his head again. Then he checked his watch and said, "Almost time. Better go hit the head." Suruga jumped off the roof and walked toward the public bathroom on the dry riverbed. Once he was out of sight of the truck, he took out his cell phone.

"This is Y286. I've acquired my target."

"How much longer to retrieve it?"

"I'll need more time to confirm its authenticity, but I should have it tonight."

"Understood. Our superiors are getting impatient, but I'll think of something to say to appease them. Were you able to confirm those two issues since we last talked?"

"On the first issue about the eyes of the shinigami—I should be able to confirm that tonight."

"And the second?"

"He's made several references to the existence of more than one L, but no conclusive evidence yet."

𝕷 13-2 Exchange

The warehouse district at night was deserted and still. The Yellow Box warehouse was apparently not in use as there were abandoned materials and old containers scattered about.

As L, Suruga, and Maki entered the warehouse, about ten men and women with rifles came out of the shadows. Secretly, Suruga was dismayed by the formation of the masked men and women that surrounded them. A circular formation was typically never employed to surround the target to avoid hitting a non-target with a stray bullet.

*You're not amateurs, for crying out loud. But I guess they have no intention of shooting us anyway. No doubt they're with the counterterrorism division like Kujo, but to think these jokers were this nation's defense against terrorism...*Suruga couldn't help but worry for Japan's security.

The man who appeared to be the leader of the group came forward. "Thank you for coming all this way. You'll have to excuse the mask." The man spoke in the same self-important, overly polite tone as on the phone. L peered through his tangled mop of hair as he rubbed the back of his bare right foot against the left.

"Well now, Mr. Ryuzaki. Shall we proceed with the exchange?"

On cue, Kujo was brought out with her hands tied behind her back.

"Dr. Kujo!" Maki shouted.

"I'm sorry this had to happen," she apologized in a barely audible voice.

Upon seeing Kujo's haggard appearance, Maki shook off L's hold on her and dashed forward. "The data's in this teddy bear. Now let go of her!"

The leader nodded, and Kujo was released.

"I'm so glad you're safe!" With her hands now free, Kujo stroked Maki's hair affectionately. Then she took the rifle from one of the men, who only a moment ago had pointed it at her, and slowly turned it on Maki.

The girl's face froze. "Dr. Kujo, why?"

Ignoring her, Kujo turned to L and said, "Mr. Ryuzaki, or shall I say Detective L? You wouldn't allow a child to hold on to the real data for this long, now would you?" Kujo pressed the barrel of the rifle to Maki's temple. Although this was L's first glimpse of Kujo's true nature, he appeared unshaken, as if he'd expected it.

"So you know." L opened his eyes wide and stuck out his tongue as if to taunt her.

"Ryuzaki! Don't give it to her! I made a promise to my father! He told me not to give it to bad people and that I had to protect the world!"

"I know. I had no intention of giving them the data from the start."

"Oh, for crying out loud!" A woman in a mask came forward, walked toward Maki with a syringe, and without the slightest hesitation, plunged it into the girl's arm.

"What do you think you're doing?" "What are you doing?" Maki and Kujo shouted at once.

Hatsune stared at the liquid remaining in the syringe and crowed, "I just made it so you'll have to hand over the data whether you want to or not. I injected the girl with the virus. Give us the data, and we'll make the antidote to save her. Without it, she won't survive past the virus's two-week incubation period. So? Now do you feel like handing over the data?"

"All right. I'll give you the real data." L stuck a hand in his jeans pocket and threw the microchip at Kujo. Picking up the microchip, which landed at her feet, she held it up to the light as if to check its contents.

"Detective L, perhaps you'd like to deduce what our next move will be, like the brilliant detective that you are." Kujo directed a challenging glare at L.

"That's hardly necessary. You have no assurances that the data I gave you is real, and yet, you won't be able to analyze its authenticity right away. Even if it were real, I would never hand over the data without making a copy for myself, in which case…"

"In which case?"

"You'd kill me where I stand and search all of my belongings."

"How very perceptive—"

Before Kujo could finish, Suruga kicked the copper pipes propped against the wall. The pipes, each five meters long, came crashing down one after the next.

"Run, Ryuzaki!"

Suruga and L made a run for it in the same direction, knocked one gang member down, and dove behind a container. They instantly drew a hail of rifle fire.

"Dammit! We're at a disadvantage being unarmed. Ryuzaki, was that the real data you gave them?"

"Yes, the data I gave them was real, but given that they have no way of knowing that, this is the correct response."

How the hell can he rationalize their actions while they're trying to kill him? Even Suruga, who knew that the gang and Kujo were on his side, was none too pleased at being shot at. *Second stage clear. And now for the third stage.*

After another bullet whistled above his head, Suruga began, "Ryuzaki, you have to write Kujo's name in the Death Note."

"In the Death Note?"

"That's right. You have it here, don't you? If we kill Kujo with it, the others will get scared enough to stop shooting."

L dropped his head in thought.

"Ryuzaki, please. Use the Death Note. At this rate, we're dead!"

Finally L looked up. "It looks like we have no other choice."

"Good, I'll draw their attention."

No sooner had he said it Suruga was on the move and dragging L with him. "Hold your fire!" Suruga's voice rang out throughout the warehouse. Using the acoustics inside the warehouse to his advantage, Suruga shouted from a location where his voice could not be pinpointed. He knew it would look bad if they couldn't even hit two stationary targets, so Suruga was on the move to make their job appear more difficult.

"What? Ready to beg for your life?" asked the leader.

"Release the girl now. Or I can't guarantee your lives," Suruga shouted, this time from a different location.

The masked members of the group scanned the area to locate the source of the voice. "I don't think you understand," the leader said. "We are the ones on the offensive, or have I misread the situation?"

"You must have heard that the Kira murders have ended. It's because L defeated him. And right now, we have Kira's killing tool in our possession."

"Killing tool?"

"That's right. The ultimate weapon capable of killing anyone as long as we know the name and face. We have it right here. Want to die right now? We know all the names of the members of your little gang."

"You're bluffing," said the leader. "Of course, I'll have to believe you if you do kill someone as you say you can."

"We have no choice but to do it, Ryuzaki. It has to be Kujo's name," Suruga said.

L nodded and produced a bag wrapped around his torso under his shirt. In it was a plain black notebook. He took the pen from Suruga and slowly began to write the name. K-U-J-O…

Just as I thought. He doesn't have the eyes of the shinigami.

The last stage of Kujo's plan had been to find out whether the Death Note was real by compelling L to use it in a life-or-death situation. Of course, they devised the strategy based on the fact that as an undercover agent, Kujo was using an alias and therefore would not die if it were written in the Death Note. The risk was the possibility that L possessed the eyes of the shinigami, which would allow him to see Kujo's real name. For this reason, Suruga had to be next to L, so he would be there to stop him should he start writing a name other than Kujo's alias.

Suruga seized the Death Note the moment L finished writing the name. "Kujo!" he called out. "Mission accomplished. I've got the Death Note, and the data you have is real." Suruga darted out waving his hands and ran to Kujo. "Ryuzaki, Maki, I'm sorry to deceive you. I was just doing my job. Forgive me."

"And now, on to stage four." Slowly, Kujo's rifle turned on Suruga. His face froze in an awkward half smile.

"What? What's going on, Kujo? These men aren't…?"

The masked members of Blue Ship laughed scornfully.

"I didn't expect you to believe that line about my being in the counterterrorism division for this long." Kujo stood on her toes to plant a kiss on Suruga's cheek. "Now we have the data and the Death Note in our possession."

The members tied up Suruga, who stood in a daze with a hand pressed to his cheek, still unable to fully grasp what was happening. After realizing Kujo had been fooling her all this time, Maki, who was still being held down, shouted, on the verge of tears, "Are you really with them, Dr. Kujo? That's like saying you killed my father!"

Kujo did not answer. Hatsune bent down instead and waved the syringe in front of her. "That's right, little girl. This lady may look shy, but she doesn't give a damn about people's lives. She's badder than this virus—"

Interrupting Hatsune, Kujo said, "Maki, do you remember our conversation in the animal husbandry room? Sometimes this world needs people to sacrifice their lives."

"Are you saying my father had to sacrifice his life for you?" Maki's cheeks flushed with anger. Kujo averted her eyes, no longer able to look at the girl.

"I'm sorry, Maki. I wanted your father to help us in our plan. But it's too late to stop now. The wheels have already been set in motion. It's just like how the destruction of the earth's environment and ecosystem can't be stopped by one person alone. It's too late for me to stop it."

"By using the virus, you're going to eliminate most of the world's population so the chosen people can create a new world?" L interjected from his hiding place. "Please tell me. You have a hostage, the Death Note, and here I am all alone, unarmed. I accept the fact that I will die here, but I'm also a detective. If I don't find out whether my deduction was correct, I won't be able to die in peace. Will you honor a dying man's wish by revealing your plan?"

"What should we do, Mr. Matoba?" Kujo turned to Matoba, unable to decide.

Matoba nodded his consent. "All right. We'll lower our guns, so come on out."

L appeared from behind the container without a hint of caution, his hands in his pockets.

"What we are trying to carry out, L, is a negative population growth plan, just as you figured. The human population has far exceeded the number the earth can adequately support. With the virus, we plan to cleanse the planet of that peril."

"It seems you have a pessimistic view of the future of mankind," L said.

A smile came across Kujo's face. "Detective L, you of all people should recognize the folly of humans. Wouldn't you agree?"

"You're right, Dr. Kujo. But I haven't lost hope in the future of mankind, and I have faith that people can change."

Kujo looked directly into L's black-rimmed panda-like eyes as if she were searching for the truth. When she realized that what L had said was not bravado but spoken from the heart, she shook her head wearily. "Such an optimist. Perhaps even a renowned detective such as yourself can't figure out the future that confronts mankind."

"How do you mean, Dr. Kujo?"

"Mankind has no future. Despite the ratification of the Kyoto Protocol to reduce CO_2 emissions, the U.S., the highest producer of carbon, abandoned the plan, while developing countries are exempt from emissions restrictions altogether. On top of which, even the ratifying countries engage in this utter farce called emissions trading, while no serious effort has been made to reduce emissions. If the CO_2 levels continue to rise, the world's major cities concentrated in coastal areas will be submerged under the sea. While people blather on about recycling and energy conservation, the time when recovery was still possible has come and gone." Kujo's voice was filled with bitterness, as if she were in the presence of a criminal trying to finish off the very life force of the earth. "The people of this world must change the way they live in a fundamental way. We have known about these problems since they were first brought to light in the '70s but have only put off confronting them. And now there's no turning back the clock."

"I appreciate the lecture, Dr. Kujo. Even so, you have no right to decide who gets to live and who gets to die. Do you really believe you'll be allowed to go through with this?"

"*Allowed* has nothing to do with it. If the population can't be controlled by natural means, then someone has to do it. Someone has to make the decision. If no one else will do it, it's up to us to maintain the balance of the natural world. That's all."

"You betrayed my father? I believed you would take over my father's mission and use the virus to bring peace to this world." Maki clenched her fist, her voice trembling.

Kujo directed the same kind smile at Maki. "While our thinking may be different from your father's, this is our best possible solution toward world peace."

"A peace that can only be gained by killing isn't real! You're no better than Kira!"

Maki's heartrending cry was enough to wipe the sneering smiles off the masked faces of the gang.

"She's right," said L. "People have the right to forge their own destinies no matter what future awaits them. Your solution to decrease the population by terrorist means is an act of pure evil."

"I wish you wouldn't confuse our plan with something so foolish and irresponsible as terrorism. We merely seek to control the number of necessary deaths and necessary lives. That's why we need the antidote. The next generation will judge whether our actions were for good or evil. Of course, you won't be alive to see that happen."

Both L and Kujo were smiling peacefully, contrary to the exchange of words between them.

"Are we about through, Detective? We really are rather busy." Matoba glanced at his watch with an exaggerated gesture.

"Of course. I'll give you the real data now." And with that, L tried to remove something from under his shirt.

"Don't—"

One of the masked men moved to stop him. But it was already too late as the object tied around L's stomach fell to the ground.

A strobe bomb. A powerful flash filled the room.

"You didn't think I would come here unprepared, did you?" L's voice echoed in a world turned completely white. Just as L had known all along, the group was not composed of hardcore terrorists, as evidenced by their awkwardness with handling weapons. Their attention had been caught by the falling bomb, and every one of them was looking directly at it when it went off.

Armed as they were, they were unable to shoot for fear of shooting one of their own. L had known the best strategy against a group of armed amateurs was to confuse them first.

The first thing Maki's eyes adjusted to was the syringe. Feeling the arms holding her down go lax, Maki shook them off, grabbed the syringe, and plunged it into Kujo's arm.

Maki's eyes burned with anger as she glared at her. "I believed you! My father died because of you! You deserve to die!"

"Maki, we're leaving." L ran up to Maki and grabbed her by the hand.

"No! I'm going to kill her. Let me go!"

Maki struggled to lunge at Kujo. The masked men regaining their sight lifted their rifles at L.

"You leave me no choice," L mumbled. He pinched the back of Maki's neck and rendered her unconscious. He darted around the warehouse carrying Maki. Obstructed by the garbage and abandoned cargo strewn about, the members of the group struggled to set their sights on a target.

For an instant, L disappeared inside a container. He held another strobe bomb in his hand when he reappeared. The pursuers again fell prey to the blinding flash. By the time their surroundings emerged into view, L and Maki were nowhere to be found.

"Damn! They got away!"

One of the members looked at the shipping slip on the container and exclaimed, "What is this container? It was delivered here today."

"To an abandoned warehouse?"

The members lowered their rifles and stared at each other, perplexed.

Taking off his mask, Matoba slicked back his hair and regarded the members of the environmental group Blue Ship. "Thank you, all. We made some progress even if it was to make the girl a carrier of the virus. World's top detective indeed. He isn't one to be dealt with lightly."

"After all, none of us are exactly trained for anything like this." Kagami, awkwardly handling his rifle, took off his mask and wiped the sweat from his face. Suruga, who was tied up, sat with his legs crossed and sulked. Hatsune flopped down in front of him and flashed him a mocking look. She paid no mind to her miniskirt, which was hiked up past well past her thighs. "Well, well, looks like L didn't bother to save you. Figures, seeing as how you betrayed him."

"Yeah, I got tired of being with him. Guess I'll be staying with you for a while. You know, your underwear's showing."

"Oh, I don't mind. There's plenty more to go around."

Kujo watched the members buzzing after the job and let out a small sigh of relief. No one noticed her being injected with the virus. Since she had been prepared to forfeit her life from the start, it was actually a blessing in disguise that she'd become a carrier. But the group's finding out about it now would be a hindrance to the plan.

Kujo collected herself and clapped her hands in their direction. "We need to move out before the police get wind of the commotion. We need to regroup and discuss our next move."

The members began to move at once.

Matoba whispered in Kujo's ear as she passed. "I was worried to see you so down as our plan progressed, but you seem to have found your enthusiasm. Is L responsible for this turnaround?"

Kujo said nothing as she approached Hatsune. "Why did you inject the girl with the virus? I told you to inject L if it became necessary,"

she said, an edge in her voice.

Hatsune ran her fingers across the sharp edge of a knife as she answered indifferently, "It's all the same result. What? Did you develop feelings for her while you were at the lab?" Pointing the stiletto knife at Kujo, she sneered, "Everyone in this country is going to die anyway."

𝕷 13-3 Hate

After escaping Yellow Box warehouse, L made a getaway in the crepe truck and parked it in the spacious lot of a pachinko parlor. After a while, Maki regained consciousness in the rear seat of the truck.

"Are you all right?" L asked her.

Maki bit her lip and stared at the mark on her arm. And L stared at her as if reading her emotional barometer.

Maki looked up and suddenly bolted for the door. But L immediately intercepted her.

"Where are you going?"

"Let go of me! I'm going to kill her! I believed her."

"If you kill Dr. Kujo out of hate, Maki, you're no better than they are."

"My father was killed in front of my eyes. Betrayed by the person I trusted the most. You don't know how it feels to lose your mother and father and be all alone."

"Yes, I do." He took out a picture of Watari he'd carried with him since his mentor's death. "I'm an orphan too. Watari, my greatest supporter, was killed by Kira. I, too, am alone in this world. That's why I understand how you feel."

"You too, Ryuzaki…?" Maki thought she detected the same inconsolable sadness in L's eyes as he stared at the picture. Troubled as she was by hearing L's past for the first time, Maki could feel her anger dissipate.

"That they injected you with the virus was unexpected." L began to work his mind, biting his nails as usual. "Suddenly we have many things we must do. We must keep the antidote from falling into the hands of the enemy, find someone who can produce the antidote to save you, and find out how the enemy intends to use the antidote. We're going to be very busy."

L's nail biting grew louder, echoing inside the truck. Maki stared at L, who seemed suddenly more alive than she'd ever seen him before.

"You seem…happy, Ryuzaki."

"Not at all." L shook his head as he started the truck. "First, we have to rescue Suruga."

Displayed on the laptop sitting on the passenger seat was a GPS with a blinking red S.

L 13-4 Spoils

"So this is the Death Note, the ultimate killing weapon."

Reluctant to put their hands on the black notebook on the table, the Blue Ship members gazed at it from afar. It did not look anything as ominous as they were expecting.

"To think you can kill anyone just by writing their name in this book…"

Kujo felt as though she were touching a gun for the first time. It was an unsettling feeling brought about by the disparity between the preciousness of life and the ease with which it could be taken away. At first, the members were suspicious of the notebook, but after Kujo explained that even the director of the FBI and president of the United States were after it, they had no choice but to acknowledge its power.

"This HOW TO USE section will make you think twice about using it." The sub-leader Yoshizawa opened the back cover and translated the English-written rules into Japanese as he read aloud. "'The person who writes a name in this notebook must continue to write a new name within thirteen days of the last or they will die.' Once you write down a name, you'll be stuck in this game of death for as long as you live."

"That's not all. 'If the notebook is rendered useless by shredding or burning, anyone who has ever touched the notebook will die.' Dang, now I wish I hadn't touched it," Hatsune said, reading over Yoshizawa's shoulder. She'd been the first one to touch the Death Note, out of curiosity.

Yoshizawa thrust the notebook in front of Konishi. "Hey, Konishi. Why don't you write down the name of someone you want dead?"

"Uh, n-no way."

Matoba, who sat at a desk removed from the rest, regretted not having handled the notebook better. Had the others not seen the rules, he could have written the name of a member who was of no particular benefit to the group, but that was impossible now that everyone had seen the notebook. Letting out a sigh, Matoba put on a leaderly face and stood up. "Our primary target was the antidote data, not the Death Note. We'll hold on to the notebook as insurance, but I can't have any of you writing in it knowing you'll die thirteen days later. If it's absolutely necessary, we can make that fool Suruga write in it."

The members laughed scornfully. Kujo stood up upon seeing their reaction.

"At this time, we will review our operation. Everyone except those who stood watch will meet here. Konishi will work on analyzing the data on the microchip. It might be embedded with a program to transmit our location, so you'll have to use a stand-alone computer."

"Understood."

The rest of the gang, fifteen members in all, gathered around Matoba and Kujo.

Kujo began, "Good work, everyone. We've come to the climax of the second phase of our plan. L's involvement was expected based on our knowledge that Nikaido had contacted L's intermediary, Watari, just before his death. With L's involvement, we predicted a 67 percent chance of success for this operation." The members nodded as they listened to Kujo's brisk explanation. Acting as Matoba's right-hand man and strategist behind the curtain, Kujo enjoyed the complete confidence of the members. "The best case scenario would have been to secure the antidote data, Maki, and the Death Note while killing L, but thanks to him, it didn't go entirely as planned. However, we did succeed in acquiring the Death Note and making the girl a carrier of the virus. As for the FBI agent…well, I don't know whether he will be useful to us as a hostage but…where is the idiot now?"

"Tied up in the storeroom," said one of the members.

"We don't have to worry about him revealing our location, do we?" Kujo asked.

"He had a transmitter in his shoe. We found it when we searched him before putting him in the car, so we're safe."

"There's really no letting your guard down with L, is there? No doubt he'll try to track our location. I want everyone to be on alert coming and going from the hideout."

"Understood."

"Mr. Konishi, how are we coming with analyzing the data?"

Konishi punched away on the computer, and after repeating the same command several times, shook his head. "Well, I couldn't find any hidden programs, but there's one program blocking access to the data that's posing a problem."

"Meaning what?"

"It's asking for a password, but if you type in the wrong one, all the data gets deleted."

Kujo pressed her right hand against her temple and shut her eyes in thought. "This could be one of L's traps. Fine. Please continue with the analysis."

"Now, will you explain what our next course of action will be?" Matoba urged.

Kujo nodded and regarded the members. "Since we no longer need to deceive Maki or Suruga, that frees us to be more direct in our methods. And now that the girl is a carrier of the virus, L will have to work on developing the antidote while the virus is still dormant. L will carry out any mission presented to him. He would never allow the girl to die."

"There are only a few facilities and scientists that can produce the antidote," said one member.

"So, we can either get the girl and produce the antidote ourselves, or wait for L to produce it and grab it," said another.

Kujo bit her lip in response to this collective overconfidence. The members of her group felt no fear or excitement at the prospect of battling the world's top detective, and that irritated her.

In fact, none of the Blue Ship, including Kujo, noticed the listening device stuck to the window.

L 12-1 Joke

Inside a shady back alley shop in Akihabara, L bought a host of mini-transmitters and various junk parts made of unknown materials. Maki compared L to the other men around them and gave a satisfied nod. "You fit right in at a place like this."

"Something tells me that's not a compliment," L said as if he might be offended, though it wasn't evident from his expression.

Down the block, L entered a maid café with the bag in his arms. A young woman in a maid costume said, "I'm sorry to keep you waiting, Master," as she brought L an ice cream sundae. He stared at her as though he had laid eyes on something inexplicable but quickly turned his attention to the sundae.

The way he held the long spoon with his fingertips—a precarious balancing act—made Maki nervous watching him, but L paid no mind as he skillfully brought the whipped cream to his mouth.

"Don't you go to elementary school, Maki?"

"Nope. I was always traveling the world with my father. But I've already completed my studies up to the eighth grade," she said proudly. But then her face clouded with doubt. "Do you think I should be going to school, Ryuzaki?"

After he pondered the question, moving his closed mouth up and down, he smiled and stuck out his tongue in an effort to reassure her.

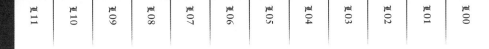

Balanced on top of his tongue was a cherry stem tied in a knot. "It's all right," he said. "I didn't go to school either."

Maki stared at him and let out a loud sigh. "Now I'm worried."

"It seems you have a knack for getting me down."

"I'm joking." She playfully thrust the back of her hand at him, like the Osakan she was, but L kept a straight face.

"I'm not good with jokes."

After finishing the sundae, L took the transmitters out of the bag, set them all to the same frequency, and covered them with duct tape. "We're ready. Let's go outside. I need your help."

The two went out into the main street and one by one began to attach the transmitters behind the license plates of the cars stopped at the traffic light.

𝓛 12-2   Rescue

"How are you feeling, Mr. Suruga?"

"Just terrific," Suruga said. "What do you want? I'm no use to you now except as a hostage…that is of course if L has any desire to save me."

Kujo held out the cell phone they'd confiscated from him.

"I thought maybe the Bureau might be expecting your call. I'd hate to have them look for you because you stopped calling. Do not let on that you've been captured or that we have the Death Note. Of course, I doubt you'd want to tell them what's happened. Now, give me the number."

Contacts' numbers were never stored and call histories always cleared for undercover cell phones in case they were stolen. She turned up the volume to maximum and waited for Suruga to tell her the number as if she'd known this. Realizing he couldn't call a random number and fake the conversation, he gave her the number.

"This is Y286."

The man who answered sounded sullen from the start. "You're late. What's happening?"

"I'm sorry. I couldn't find a moment alone."

"Again with the excuses. You said you'd acquire the target last night."

"That might take some more—"

"I'm tired of hearing it. The only reason you were chosen for this assignment was because you had a reasonable motive for approaching L with your personal connections to Raye and Naomi. If you're not making progress, most of us are of the opinion that we should take a different tact. Just what the hell are you doing now?"

"…Trying to win L's trust," Suruga said.

Kujo stared at him with an amused look as Suruga labored to make excuses.

"Fine. It's progress enough that you were able to find the real Death Note. We're moving on to a different strategy. You need to distance yourself from L and come back in."

"Uh…wait!"

The man hung up without hearing Suruga's protest.

"Poor L. He has Maki, a virus carrier, to look after, and now he's being hunted by us and the FBI."

Suruga glowered at Kujo's mock sympathy. "But if the FBI captures L, the girl will automatically be put under police protection. Then you won't be able to lay a hand on either of them. Too bad."

It was Suruga's best attempt at bravado, but the smile on Kujo's face remained. "I appreciate the concern. But you didn't think we would execute our plan without anticipating that, did you?"

†

Upon Kujo's return, Konishi drew closer to the computer screen and said quizzically, "A malfunction…?"

The screen went white like a halation and moments later, a calligraphic letter faded up onscreen.

"Hey, on this computer too! This isn't…"

The letter L appeared on the monitors of all four computers in the room.

"To the members of Blue Ship, thank you for your hospitality last night," said an electronically altered voice coming through the speakers of every one of the computers.

"L! How did you…?" Kujo was paralyzed, her face ashen.

"How did I find your location? That's because I'm L," he answered simply, as if no further explanation were necessary. "There's something else I know—all of your names. Daisuke Matoba, Tamotsu Yoshizawa, Hatsune Misawa. It seems you've made quite a name for yourselves overseas as well."

"So what if you know our names? We have the Death Note," Yoshizawa said to the closest computer screen.

"I have in my possession another Death Note."

The Blue Shippers froze.

"Another Death Note?"

"You're all familiar with the second Kira from the Sakura TV incident? There were two Kiras and thus also two Death Notes in existence. I have in my possession the second Death Note."

"What do you want, Ryuzaki, no…L?" asked Matoba, who'd been listening quietly.

"Release Suruga."

Matoba shook his head as though it were out of the question. "Do you really think we would give up our valuable hostage?"

"Mr. Matoba, I rather appreciate a person who is quick to understand. I know your names and faces. You, however, do not know my name. There is only one choice. Am I right?"

Matoba grimaced at having his own words from the other night thrown back at him. "But L, Mr. Suruga betrayed you. Why do you want to save him?"

"I plan to do no such thing."

"Now you're contradicting yourself. If you have no intention of saving him, then what do you mean by demanding his release?"

"I want him so I can exact retribution with my own hands. If I can't confirm his release in the next ten minutes, Mr. Matoba, you will die first."

†

"Ryuzaki, I'm sorry."

After his release, Suruga boarded the crepe truck and bowed his head dejectedly.

"About what?" L took the wheel like nothing was the matter and started the truck after checking to see if they were being followed.

"You know, for getting close to you without revealing my true intentions, for being fooled by Kujo—"

"No. Thank you."

"Huh?"

L flashed a mischievous smile as he held out *taiyaki* on a stick. "Thanks to you and Dr. Kujo, I was able to learn your real intentions, Dr. Kujo's true identity, and the group she's working with. And in a way that was convincing to Maki."

It was too much for Suruga to take in at once. But now that he thought about it, the signs had been there: the disparity between his and Kujo's security checks, the absence of cameras in the server room...As he looked back on it now, everything had been pre-arranged to make a partnership between him and Kujo possible. "How did you find their hideout anyway? They took the transmitter from my shoe."

"That transmitter was a dummy. The real one is in there." L pointed to Suruga's stomach.

"Huh? My stomach?! Hey, you didn't..."

Before they had gone to Yellow Box warehouse, Suruga had complained of stomach pains from drinking too much of the sweet coffee, for which L had given him a pill.

"I put a transmitter in a non-dissolving capsule. You should probably do something to expel it later."

So making me drink that coffee was all part of the plan, Suruga thought, rubbing his stomach.

"After locating the Blue Ship hideout, I planted a listening device and watched the building from a hotel room nearby to confirm the faces of the group members. I used your ID to access the FBI's network and ran a crosscheck of the criminal data."

Suruga nearly let that last part sail by before he hastily looked up and said, "But my ID—"

"Of course, I used the ID and password under your real name, Hideaki Sugita," L said offhandedly.

"Th-then, what about the strobe bombs at the Yellow Box warehouse? I was with you the whole time since the attack. When did you have time to get them?" This time, L shot him a sideways glance and did not answer. "What, you want me to figure it out? Now wait a minute..."

Suruga thought about it as he rubbed the growth on his chin. It would have been impossible to obtain the bomb after the attack on the Kira Investigation building. But if it was possible to know the location of the hideout before the attack... "You weren't eavesdropping on my conversations with Kujo in the server room, were you? There weren't any cameras or bugs in that room."

"I heard a conversation, but I wasn't eavesdropping."

"What is that supposed to mean?"

"I forgot one of my cell phones in the server room, and when I called the number, I happened to hear you talking with Dr. Kujo. So it wasn't eavesdropping."

So basically he turned the tables on us. Suruga almost bit his nails but hastily lowered his hand, avoiding imitating L.

"I hacked into the systems of an explosives manufacturer, shipping company, and port administration offices and had a shipping container delivered to the warehouse before the time of the exchange."

Suruga was beyond shocked and could only laugh. "I give up. You saw through everything from the start."

"That's because I'm L," he said simply. Of course, such words only a man with the title of world's top detective could utter, but there was not a hint of pride in the declaration—only more loneliness.

Suddenly Suruga recalled the image of L playing chess alone. *That knight moving back and forth across the board...that was me,* he realized only now.

"After we closed the Kira investigation, I submitted a report to the FBI, and then you suddenly appeared. It would be strange not to be suspicious. I knew from the beginning that you had approached me to investigate and recover the Death Note. And that you would probably use an alias to guard against its powers."

L pulled the truck over to the side of the road and turned around to check on Maki in the back seat. Hugging the teddy bear to her chest, she whispered "Daddy" in her sleep. L looked up as though he remembered something and put a blanket over her. He might have been reminded of that fatherly figure who used to do the same for him.

"The only part I failed to anticipate was that they would inject Maki with the virus. Not only do we have to protect the antidote data, now we must produce the antidote before Maki begins to manifest the symptoms. We don't have very many options."

"On the other hand, the enemy's options just increased. They could steal the antidote data or wait for us to make the drug and steal that."

*Because of me...*A chagrined smile crossed Suruga's face.

"But the situation isn't entirely bad. Originally the enemy was in the position of making any demand they wanted, virtually holding the world hostage with the virus. But now that we know their names and faces, we can put a stop to their actions. And it's all thanks to your getting caught."

"Like a blessing in disguise, eh? But Kujo hinted at having more tricks up her sleeve, so better not let our guard down."

"Mr. Suruga, would you mind assisting me for a while longer? It would be a great help to me if you were around."

A help? You must be joking, Suruga thought, but he had already made up his mind. "Of course, I'll help. It was because I was fooled by Kujo that Maki was injected with the virus. And besides, the Bureau took me off the assignment of investigating you."

As Suruga took over at the wheel, he felt a touch of uneasiness. *Maybe turning me over to the enemy was part of L's plan. Not only to use me as a pawn but to make me feel beholden to him later...*

†

"It could be me, but something's not right. Maybe they anticipated that we'd come back here."

Suruga leaned forward in the driver's seat. They were nearing the Kira Investigation Headquarters to gather some supplies they'd need to face the enemy. It was like any other night in Tokyo, with taxis speeding by and overworked businessmen trudging the streets after putting in hours of overtime. But Suruga felt a palpable tension in the air. Parking the truck in a blind spot, they scanned the area first before Suruga and L left Maki behind in the truck and approached the Kira Investigation Headquarters.

Suddenly two men in full helmets attacked from out of the shadows. Falling forward on his hands instinctively, Suruga stopped one

man's advance with an upward kick to the shoulder, twisted his upper body in the same motion and landed a hard kick to the face. With that, one man was out cold.

The other raised his club and attacked L, who inexplicably fell over on his back like an overturned frog. The best strategy against trained professionals was the element of surprise. Unless the enemy was a seasoned veteran with extensive combat experience, unpredictable moves as this one typically caused him to hesitate for a split second. Seizing the opportunity, L grabbed an umbrella off the ground and hooked the curved handle around the man's leg. Although the man did not fall over, it was enough to slow him down. In the meantime, Suruga maintained his momentum from dispatching his man and grabbed L's attacker and threw him to the ground, ripping off his helmet in the process.

"You're—"

The man let out a yelp, frightened that his face had been exposed.

With the hint of people drawing near to investigate the commotion, Suruga and L fled the scene and ran back to the truck.

"Damn! The FBI's changed their strategy because they didn't think I was getting anywhere with my investigation. But attacking one of their own!"

"They were sent to recover the Death Note. The full helmets were to protect against the possibility that I possessed the eyes of the shinigami."

"I suppose they're after me for collaborating with you against orders. Now we have to run from the FBI and Blue Ship!" Suruga lamented aloud and began to drive. "Ryuzaki, you used to run a joint investigation with the Metropolitan Police. What if you talked to them and asked for their cooperation?"

Perched on top of the passenger seat, L stated unequivocally, "No, I won't rely on the police, or any other agencies for that matter for this mission."

"What's got into you? Dispatching the police and intelligence agencies of the world as your pawns, relegating others to bear the brunt, never revealing yourself to others—that's always been the way you operated."

Of all the cases L had solved in the past, not one was credited to him on the official record. The Los Angeles BB Murder Cases, during which he had used Naomi as his pawn, was typical. (In reality, by using the name Ryuzaki and hundreds of other detective codes, L alone was more active than the average private detective agency.) For L, as long as his relative safety was directly connected with the security of the world, this was the way it had to be. However, the reality was that the investigative and intelligence agencies had grown suspicious of L and had come to regard him as a secretive and selfish detective who bore none of the risk.

For a minute, L stared down at his broken watch. His usual expressionless face gave way to a sad smile.

"My only friend once told me…that I knew nothing of the real world, having locked myself inside a room. Which is precisely why I'd like to complete this mission without depending on any of the organized agencies. But this is just my selfish desire. If you wish to leave, Mr. Suruga, now is your chance."

For a while Suruga was quiet as he gripped the wheel. Then he turned to look at Maki balled up asleep in the back and let out a resigned sigh. "Looks like all three of us are on the run now. I'm dedicating this one to Raye and Naomi. Let's do this right."

An FBI car closed in on them from behind.

—Turn left ahead.—

The crepe truck's recommended route was to drive in the wrong direction down a narrow one-way street.

"It's the FBI who are after us now. The level of difficulty just went up," L said matter-of-factly.

Suruga made a hard right onto the street. The oncoming cars bore down on them.

"Gah!" Suruga desperately jerked the wheel from side to side, while L sat calmly next to him.

"By the way, what was that kicking technique you used before?"

"Oh, that? It's called capoeira. A guy from South America gave me a few pointers. It's a practical martial art."

"Interesting moves. Will you teach them to me later?"

The FBI car did not hesitate to chase them the wrong way down the one-way street and drew closer. Suruga drove the truck up the sidewalk, leveling the chairs in an open café, and answered, "Let's lose these jokers first!"

†

Back at the Blue Ship hideout, the members eyed each other gravely after having been forced to release Suruga.

"What are we doing going up against the likes of the world's top detective? At this rate, who knows when all of our names will be found out and written in the Death Note?" said one of the men, frightened. "Even if we do have the killer virus, we won't be able to use it as leverage now. The moment we use the virus, Mr. Matoba's and Yoshizawa's names will be written in the book."

Kujo contemplated their next move, even as she was kicking herself for not anticipating the possibility that two notebooks might exist. Though the group's goal was to obtain antidote data, right now their priority was to guard against the Death Note.

"Fortunately, we still have Nikaido's cell phone. As long as we can use it to track Maki's location, L is sure to be there as well. If we attack quickly without giving him the opportunity to write a name, we can neutralize the Death Note."

The Blue Ship members nodded.

"Dr. Kujo, about the GPS in the girl's cell phone..." Konishi said

in a troubled voice as he stared at the computer screen.

"What is it?"

"Take a look at this."

Displayed on the GPS onscreen were over 50 red blinking dots indicating the frequency of Maki's cell phone, all moving in different directions on the map.

"What is this?" Kujo asked quizzically. "Are the settings right?"

The other members peered at the screen.

Konishi replied, "It's likely L stuck transmitters set to the same frequency as the girl's cell phone onto random cars."

Everyone fell silent when they realized that L had been steps ahead of them yet again. They were struck dumb by the hard reality of matching wits against the world's top detective.

After taking a moment to think, Kujo raised her head and directed a determined look at Matoba. Then she asked, "Mr. Matoba, may I set the next plan in motion?"

Matoba, who had been listening on as he admired the biotope, nodded with a magnanimous air.

"The next plan?" The needy eyes of the members focused on Kujo.

"It's time we stopped playing detective trying to hunt down L. We'll leave that to the experts. By exploiting the fact that L is on the run with a virus carrier."

"But if we're not careful, he might write our names in the Death Note." One younger member did not even try to hide his fear.

"Don't worry," Kujo reassured him. "We'll drive them into a situation where L won't have the time to remember our names."

L 11 News

"Professor Kishikawa of Tohoku University…and he would be able to produce the antidote?"

"Probably. My father was in contact with him."

"Tohoku University should have the necessary equipment to do it."

L and Maki were on the Yamanote Line train. L had kicked his shoes off and was crouched atop the seat as usual. As unsteady as this posture was, he skillfully kept his balance on the rocking train with a Chupa Chups in one hand. The young man sitting opposite them shot him a dubious glance even as he played with his cell phone indifferently.

"Then let's head for our destination. Just the two of us, without anyone else's assistance." L held up the Chupa Chups as if it were the destination to which they were headed. Maki stared at him as though she had laid eyes on a strange animal.

"Why are you doing all this for me?"

"It's because this will be my last job."

"Last…what do you mean?"

He looked at Maki with the lollipop bulging in his right cheek. He seemed to smile behind the black-rimmed insomniac eyes.

"I wrote my own name in the Death Note in order to end my

battle with Kira," L said in his usual monotone. "I have eleven more days to live. It's the very same length of time you have."

Maki's eyes widened. "Aren't you afraid to die? I am. I'm terrified." Maki shook her head as if to shake off the fear. "Why are you trying to save me and the world when you only have days to live yourself?"

"I will continue to do what I must until the very last moment. That's all."

"Those are the same words..." Maki thought she saw her father in L's profile. "It's what my father used to say all the time. He used to say never to lose sight of what you have to do, no matter what troubles come your way. He used to worry if what he was doing was really helping people. But as long as there were people suffering and dying, he told me that somebody had to do the job."

"He sounds like an extraordinary man."

Maki nodded shyly.

L looked out the window as if to recall feelings he himself didn't know he had. "I never knew my parents. But recently, I've come to know someone whom I've grown to respect as a father. Your father must have been that kind of man. I would have liked to meet him."

The figure that came into L's mind might have been that of Soichiro Yagami, who had believed in his son's innocence, yet stuck to his principles and protected the law in deciding to arrest his son as a serial killer.

"What I have to do..." Maki murmured as if to convince herself of something.

The young man sitting across from them continued to fiddle with his cell phone. He glanced idly at the breaking-news bulletin on the news site he'd been watching to pass the time.

—A girl suspected of being infected with a new strain of virus has escaped the hospital. Anyone who has seen this girl is being urged to notify the police immediately and to be checked at the nearest hospital to see if

they have been infected.—

The young man's eyes drifted above the phone screen to the pair sitting before him. The girl in the picture and the girl sitting in front of him were one and the same.

"No way…"

The businessman next to him looked over the young man's shoulder at the screen. After eyeing the girl's picture and the words "New Virus Outbreak" scrolling beneath it, he looked to where the young man was now staring.

"Oh God!" the man shouted as he shot to his feet. He barreled past the other passengers into the next car. The passengers began to stir.

"No way. No frickin' way!" the young man repeated and dropped his cell phone. L saw the picture of Maki on the phone, which tumbled his way, and immediately understood what was happening. Picking the phone up off the ground, Maki stood up to hand it back to its owner.

"Get away! Get away from me!" The man cried and flopped to the floor in a panic when Maki took a step in his direction. He practically crawled out when the train stopped and opened its doors at a station; his cell phone and belongings remained where he left them. Confused, Maki noticed the picture of herself on the screen and went into shock.

"We can't use public transportation anymore. Let's go." Taking Maki by the hand, L got off the train at Shibuya Station and descended the stairs. As they navigated the intersection swarming with people, L noticed that Maki had slowed her pace. When he looked behind him, she was staring up at something in a daze.

Her face was being displayed on a JumboTron on the side of a building.

"Try to keep your head down, Maki." L tried to cover her face as he grabbed her hand and started running again. "This country has a manual for dealing with these things, but they're usually so busy assigning blame that their response comes much later. This time, however, their response was unexpectedly fast. It seems I underestimated Dr. Kujo."

The look on Maki's face remained vacant as though she had not heard him. Her head was filled with the cruel reality that even now the deadly virus was multiplying inside her body in preparation for the onset of the symptoms. Maki was aware of how people infected with a hemorrhagic fever virus died. Along with developing a fever, their entire body became covered with pustules until finally, they died, spurting blood out of every orifice. It was a picture of hell.

"Am I going to die?"

"Don't worry. I'll protect you."

L took out a Chupa Chups from his pocket and offered it to Maki. They ran under the rail bridge and continued on down a narrow side street.

話 10-1 Surrounded

"Just what were you thinking, Dr. Kujo? Thanks to your grand-standing, the place is in absolute chaos," accused Saegusa, an elderly professor in charge of the Pandemic Task Force at the Ministry of Health, Labour, and Welfare. "How dare you issue a warning about an escaped viral patient over the airwaves without consulting the Infectious Disease Countermeasures Network first. And not by Pro-fessor Nikaido himself, but by you, a representative. Anyone with common sense—"

"We are in a race against time," Kujo interrupted Saegusa, who spoke as he wiped his glasses. "What would have happened if we consulted you first? There would have been endless meetings over whether or not to announce the threat of the virus and over who would accept the responsibility of doing so. In fact, how long did it take you to summon me here?"

"Action is to be taken when all the necessary preparations have been made. In the end, that is the most effective way to proceed."

But Kujo dismissed such a Japanese way of thinking. "I am merely pointing out this country's lack of crisis management skills when it comes to infectious diseases."

"What's done is done," said Saegusa. "But Dr. Kujo, after all your requests for information over the airwaves, we have yet to receive any information about the girl. Is there really such a girl on the run?"

The members of the task force looked toward Kujo at once. They were the stereotypical Japanese corporate drones who, while loath to bear any responsibility themselves, obsessed with finding blame in others.

Kujo faced them as a way to repel their stares. "The girl who was infected is Professor Nikaido's daughter. She was accidentally infected with the new strain of virus her father had been researching."

"Did you conceal how she was infected and lie about her escaping a hospital to protect Professor Nikaido?"

"I couldn't go public with the truth because Professor Nikaido was the one who smuggled the virus into Japan in the first place. The professor was involved with a terrorist organization and was planning to take part in a viral terrorist attack. We think his daughter was infected in the process."

"Not Professor Nikaido…" one of the task force members said in disbelief.

"As you know, Nikaido Research Lab is a biosafety level four facility, but it's prohibited from handling viruses above level three per an agreement with residents in the area. Nevertheless, the virus was smuggled into the lab, and the lab's director who was plotting a viral terrorist attack has gone missing. And now his daughter, a carrier of the virus, has escaped. Do you really think we can report the truth, such as it is?"

The task force members averted their eyes at once, reluctant to get involved. They began to speak in hushed tones with the person next to them, not one willing to propose a solution that could be put into action.

"What is the transmission risk of the virus?" one member asked after collecting himself.

"It has both a transmission risk and fatality rate higher than that of the Ebola virus. And after the two-week incubation period, it will multiply at an explosive rate."

"How does it...?" Saegusa hesitated to ask the question.

"It's an airborne virus," Kujo answered soberly.

The conference room fell silent again. The virus could spread from the host's phlegm, cough, and vomit and enter the new host's lungs. This was a virus with an extremely high fatality rate, which was also capable of spreading exponentially.

"What would you like to do? Will you allow this country to be wiped out or will you establish a task force immediately?"

No one uttered a word. Finally Saegusa relented. "We have no choice. We'll have to set up a task force. And I expect you to take part, Dr. Kujo."

Even as Kujo nodded with a hard look on her face, she was trying desperately to keep from laughing at the performance Saegusa was putting on.

†

Konishi took one look at Kujo who returned to the hideout and smiled. "I take it everything went well."

"Yes, I was brought onto the task force without any problem. It will be set up inside the Ministry of Health, Labour, and Welfare."

Kujo took off her coat and fixed her eyes on the biotope in the center of the room.

"I gather the information about Saegusa's collusive activities with a pharmaceutical company was useful." Matoba's voice came from the other end of the biotope.

"Yes, it was all I could do to keep from laughing."

"So the girl will be captured soon enough. You were right, the job of catching her should be left up to the experts. What with this still going on..." Konishi glanced at the dozens of red dots scattered across the map of Japan and threw his hands up in surrender.

"Yes, but I want you to continue working on locating the girl's GPS."

"Huh? Why is that?"

"We still want to get to the girl first. Any witness reports we receive go directly to the task force. I'll leak the vital information to you here so you can use it to pinpoint Maki's GPS."

"What happens if the police get to her first?"

"Once she's found, she will have to be quarantined. Since the hospital won't know how to treat this new strain of virus, they will defer treatment to the task force."

"In either case, the girl will end up in our hands," Matoba murmured. He gazed complacently at the harmonious world contained inside the biotope. "The day that this ideal world will become reality is at hand."

Kujo contemplated the biotope. But her gaze soon drifted to the distorted profile of Matoba reflected in the glass.

"An ideal world…"

No one noticed the cynical smile that crossed Kujo's lips.

ɮ 10-2 Cybernet

A young woman with a coffee cup rang the bell on the counter of the Internet café. Excuse me, you're out of sugar," she called out.

The part-timer ambled out of the back and began to refill the bins with packets of sugar. He mumbled, "Geez, I just refilled it."

The Internet café was nearly filled to capacity. As crowded as it was in the middle of the night, the café was quiet save for the occasional cough or snore. The silence seemed heightened by the alienation of customers closed off in private cubicles even as they shared a common network between them.

One cubicle was occupied by two customers wearing Hanshin Tigers caps. They might have been brothers separated only by age. The younger brother was buried in a blanket, asleep. The older brother sat on the loveseat with his legs folded tightly against his chest and worked on the computer. Though this posture looked unsteady, he kept his balance, gripping the edge of the sofa with his bare feet, like an eagle clutching a branch with its talons. What he had up onscreen was neither an online game nor an adults-only site. Operating the two computers in the cubicle as well as his own laptop, the man took in the information scrolling across three monitors, all crowded with open browser windows, at once.

The Metropolitan Police Department, Ministry of Health, Labour, and Welfare, each of the regional police departments. All of the information being accessed was from internal confidential files closed to the general public. One after the next, the man typed away on each of the screens.

Five coffee cups and countless packets of sugar were set next to the keyboard. The man's eyes did not once stray from the computer screen as he poured packet after packet of sugar into the cup. The man should have just ordered a cup of sugar with a splash of coffee. The man gulped down the tan sludge and smacked his lips. "Dee-licious!" he said to nobody but himself.

As he continued to type away with cup in hand, he glanced occasionally at the laptop on the sofa. There were two sites displayed onscreen.

The first, titled Challenge: Once Around Japan, was a site for young adventurers traveling Japan by foot, bicycle, or motorcycle to post their current destinations for others to track. As summer vacation had started, messages such "Leaving Osaka today!" and "Heading for Hakodate. Meet me at the convenience store in front of train station" were being posted despite the late hour.

And the other was the website dedicated to Misa Amane, who recently resumed her entertainment career. The events pages listed the various summer festivals around the country at which she was scheduled to appear.

"Misa Amane: forfeited ownership of the Death Note and lost all memory of the notebook. The only memory that remains is her love for Light Yagami…"

The man's younger brother rolled over in his sleep and moaned like he was having a nightmare. His forehead dripped with sweat.

"Is something the matter?" When the older brother shook him awake, the kid jumped up, kicked the blanket aside, and let out a sigh of relief.

"It's nothing," The younger brother shook his head and took off the Tigers cap to wipe the sweat from his face. A bundle of long hair came tumbling down his, no, *her* face.

Although Maki tried to act cheerful, she had not slept well these last couple of days and was routinely startled awake out of her nightmares. It was clear she was fighting the fear of the onset of the virus. L stared at Maki as he bit his nails, perhaps frustrated by his inability to do anything for her.

There was another voice at the counter, and it did not sound like it belonged to a customer. Opening the door of his cubicle, L peeked out. Leaning against the counter was a policeman. As a late-night gathering place of unspecified types, the café was a regular stop for the police, but this did not appear to be a routine stop.

"Geez, I just got on at midnight, and I can't remember every face that comes through here," said the irritated part-timer. He didn't bother to look at the picture the policeman held up.

"Anyway, I'm going to have a look around," the policeman said forcefully. He started his walk around the café.

"Maki, it's the police. We have to leave," urged L as he fixed the baseball cap on his head.

L ducked down and carefully undid all but one of latches holding the wall of the cubicle together, then tilted the wall from the rim so that the bottom lifted up. Maki crawled underneath, followed quickly by L. They hid under the computer desk in the dark and empty cubicle next to theirs until the policeman passed them by, and then crawled past the counter at the entrance and broke into a dash out the door. It was then the policeman finally noticed and ran after them.

When L and Maki burst through the door, they were quickly intercepted by the other police officer waiting outside. L caught his leg on the chain roping off the parking lot and fell. As he started to get up, he kicked up his legs and hit the policeman squarely in the jaw, sending him head over heels on the ground with a wild capoeira move. A stunned look flashed across his face for an instant, then the policeman took off after them again.

"That looked too good to be an accident," Maki said, running.

"I should say inevitable. It was just as I planned."

Maki stared dubiously at L, who looked a little proud of himself.

"Did you get everything done back at the café?"

"Yes, we can move on to our next plan. Over there!" he said, pointing toward the train station. They ran to the entrance, and L began to survey the bicycles that lined the racks in front of the train station.

"Huh? We're going by bike? Just how far do you think we're going?"

L paid no mind as he picked out an electrically assisted bicycle, undid the combination lock without any problem, and wheeled the bicycle into the shadows of a building. Taking out a control board as well as various parts he'd bought in Akihabara from his knapsack, he got to work on modifying the bicycle.

"By the way, what does the mark on our caps mean?" L asked.

"What do you mean, it's the Hanshin Tigers logo. The baseball team in Osaka?"

"And the cap with the 'G' on it was no good?"

When he was shopping for caps, he had picked out a cap with a "G" on it bearing the logo for the rival Yomiuri Giants, which Maki had swatted out of his hand.

"You have to root for Hanshin if you're born in Osaka!"

"Do you know someone on the team?"

"What do you mean?"

"I have never rooted for someone I don't know just because the team represents my hometown. It's an odd custom."

Maki gave L an exasperated look. "Ryuzaki, you might be real smart but you really should study up on people's feelings."

"I get that a lot," said L with a frown as he continued to work on the bicycle.

"I've completed the modifications. Hop on back." The bicycle slid forward carrying the two of them and quickly picked up speed.

"What did you do to modify...w-whoa! No bicycle should be this fast!" Maki held on to L's waist and gasped for air.

"I made a modification to the motor control board by adjusting torque so that the bicycle thinks it's continually going uphill. Now I don't even have to pedal."

L 10-3 Counterattack

Inside the headquarters of the Pandemic Task Force, doctors called in from hospitals around Tokyo that were besieged with phone calls.

"No, as I told you, the symptoms you described are not consistent with those of the virus. Please have it checked out at your local hospital. Yes ma'am. Calm down, it's all right."

"Even the measles and chicken pox are being mistaken for the symptoms of the virus."

"What directions should we give to the hospitals turning away children with high fevers?"

Kujo, having just arrived, gave out precise directives to the helpless doctors. "If the patient has a fever over 102 degrees and does not develop a rash on the face, arms, or legs two hours after onset, the patient has not been infected with the virus. Tell them that."

Information about suspicious individuals came in at a steady stream from checkpoints set up across the country. Though charged with overseeing the operations of the task force, Kujo examined the stacks of reports in search of something. "At 0:37, male, 20s, and female child sighted at Internet café in Saitama City..." Kujo read aloud. "1:23, apprehended male, 20s, and female child who fled the scene after questioning in Hasuda City...2:55, individual threatened to infect policeman at checkpoint at Shiraoka, fled the scene on bicycle..."

Kujo snuck out of the room with her cell phone and headed up to the roof of the building. After making sure no one else was around, she called Yoshizawa at the Blue Ship hideout. "We received a report that sounds like them. They're headed north out of Saitama City. Probably on bicycle at this speed."

"On the run on a bicycle. Sounds like they're getting desperate. North out of Saitama City...just as we expected."

"Yes, they appear to be heading for Sendai. The girl must know that Nikaido was friendly with Professor Kishikawa at Tohoku University. He's probably the only one they can ask to produce the antidote. We should grab them before they reach the checkpoint at Kuki City. Leave only the minimum number of members to watch over Nikaido's lab and home, and send the rest to Kuki City."

"Understood."

Kujo hung up and returned to the headquarters. As she continued to expedite the calls that came in quick succession, she worked out several contingencies in the back of her mind. There were three possible scenarios: one in which they pinpoint Maki's GPS and grab L and Maki before the checkpoint; another in which L and Maki are apprehended at the checkpoint and taken to a hospital; and another in which they safely reach Professor Kishikawa at Tohoku University. Kujo had already made the necessary preparations for all three possibilities. They had already tightened the screws on Kishikawa so he would cooperate.

But something stuck in Kujo's mind. Telling herself that she was just being overly anxious, Kujo resumed checking the new reports coming in.

—*0:30, male, 20s, and male child fled Internet café in Adachi Ward.*—

After studying this report for a moment, she rifled through the stacks for the first report she'd seen and compared them. "Male child...the possibility that Maki is disguised...a decoy?" Kujo mumbled just as her cell phone vibrated.

She hurried to the roof again and hit the talk button. Yoshizawa shouted, "We've been had!" on the other end.

"What happened?"

"We tracked the GPS we thought was L and Maki, but when we caught up with them, it wasn't them. It was some random kid traveling the country by bicycle. He didn't know where he got stuck with the transmitter."

Kujo ended the call, clucked her tongue, and headed for the underground garage.

"If it was a decoy, was it designed to throw us off their scent? Maybe Suruga and L are moving separately...and with different goals?" she said to herself. Kujo's car peeled out of the garage and ran every traffic light as it sped down the dark night road.

†

"Ryuzaki's probably saying how everything's going as planned about now. Never mind that," Suruga muttered as he hid in the bushes outside the Blue Ship hideout and wiped the sweat trickling down his face. "Is this what they call global warming? Kujo's ideal world must be one cool place to live."

Although Suruga was used to warm weather, he'd grown tired of the muggy, windless, and mosquito-filled nights in Japan. "Damn! I could've taken these bastards down in a minute with a partner or two. But I guess I can only blame myself for that."

Suruga couldn't very well inform the Bureau that he had failed to recover the Death Note from L, much less confess that it had been stolen away by a third party. And now that he'd been taken off the assignment, he could no longer ask for the Bureau's help. At the moment, he was moving separately from L and Maki. Suruga was on his own, but he still spoke aloud.

"The truck ought to start rolling soon."

Suruga had parked the truck he'd stolen just up the hill—without pulling the emergency brake. Wheel chocks made of ice were set in front of the tires. The ice barely lasted ten minutes on top of the scorching asphalt, which still retained the heat from the midday sun. When the chocks melted, the truck began to lurch forward. The truck gained speed and barreled down the hill, stopping only when it crashed into a utility pole and knocked it down. Suddenly the area went dark.

Suruga had already confirmed that the building that Blue Ship was using as a hideout was not equipped with an emergency generator.

"Mission start: 03:21."

Suruga entered through the front of the building and ran up the stairs, hitting the emergency alarm as he passed it.

"I'm coming in!"

Using the Russian military-issue night vision goggles he'd pro-cured from a black market shop, he allowed one panicked member to blow past him, then he bowed before entering the room.

While Blue Ship might have been regarded as a terrorist group, its members were nothing more than amateurs. With the sudden darkness and emergency alarm, they froze in panic. And because most of the members had cleared out thanks to L's plan, there was no one to give orders.

"It might be a trap. Guard the Death Note!" Suruga shouted to incite further confusion. When the enemy's chain of command was confused, exploit it by making the enemy work for you—that was a fundamental plan of attack. "Is the notebook safe?" Suruga shouted again. Moving quickly, he took up a position in a corner of the room to observe the action.

"It's right here!" one thug answered from another corner of the room. He waved a briefcase over his head.

Without a word Suruga crept up next to him. Covering the man's mouth and nose, Suruga slammed him against the wall and kicked him in the solar plexus. The man groaned in pain, the noise drowned out by the alarm.

With the briefcase in hand, Suruga quietly snuck out of the room and descended the stairs. Upon exiting the building, he removed the night vision goggles and checked his watch. "Mission accomplished: 03:26. Required time: five minutes. Not bad," he said.

"It's not over yet, Mr. Suruga."

Kujo stood in his path, a gun in her hand.

"You don't mean to shoot me in this residential area, now do you? With the accident and blackout, people are already coming outside. The police will start snooping around soon enough. Fortunately, the only thing I've got on me is a notebook. Still going to shoot, Kujo?"

Kujo smiled and lowered the gun. "And I believed you and I would make a good team," Kujo said, without a hint of remorse. She drew closer and smiled at Suruga as if her treachery had already been forgotten.

"You're one to talk after the way you fooled me. You scare me."

"If I scare you so much, perhaps you shouldn't make an enemy of me." Kujo's hand brushed against his. Though it was a sweltering night, the fingers twining around his were cold.

Suruga sensed the snare of her grip closing and brushed her hand aside. "It all comes down to who'd make a scarier enemy—you or L." Suruga waved and turned to go.

"Then brace yourself, Mr. Suruga. Or should I say, Hideaki Sugita," Kujo said in a voice that was frightfully calm.

"How do you know that name?"

"L isn't the only one who knows how to investigate people." Kujo was no longer looking at Suruga. Instead, her eyes were trained on L and Maki, the pair of whom had just arrived. "I'm so sorry, Maki. I never imagined that you would be infected—"

"Tell me, Dr. Kujo. Are you really going to use the virus to destroy the world?" Maki interrupted.

"No. I'm trying to build a new world—"

"By killing people?"

Kujo fell silent. The two, who once trusted each other like family, kept their distance, the gap between them physical as well as emotional.

"I wouldn't be happy living in a peaceful world that was created by sacrificing people's lives," Maki said.

Kujo faltered for a moment, but then began again. "Maki, of course that's the ideal. A world where everyone can laugh and live happily. But that isn't possible now. You should know that after traveling the world with your father."

This time it was Maki's turn to fall silent. She recalled the countless countries and regions she'd been to with her father. Even a child like Maki recognized the conflicts and problems that had befallen the earth, problems the planet could not handle.

"Maki, do you remember what we talked about in the animal husbandry room? The reason you can live a healthy life is because those research animals sacrifice their lives. Sacrifice is a necessary part of any accomplishment."

"And you're satisfied with that? I don't believe that's how you really feel."

Kujo bit her lip and answered quietly, "No, this is how I feel. I only worked with Professor Nikaido to liberate the virus, for the good of the planet."

Maki stared at Kujo as though she were trying to ascertain her true intentions. She let out a deep sigh. "It looks like I had you all wrong, Dr. Kujo." Something between them ended with those words.

"Ryuzaki, Maki, the power will be back on soon. We should go," Suruga said.

L, who had been watching this exchange between Maki and Kujo, finally said, "Dr. Kujo, what you are attempting to do under the pretext of building an ideal society is nothing more than mass murder. If you carry out this plan, I will kill you. You will be—" L took a step forward—"executed!"

Then he handed the woman a lollipop.

†

"You look like everything went as expected. Are you telling me that you knew that if we split up, I would try to get the Death Note back?" Suruga asked as the trio walked together through the dark streets of town.

L said nothing but smiled mischievously. Perhaps it was because L respected Suruga's infiltration skills that he'd made such a prediction, which Suruga couldn't feel too badly about.

"Then were you expecting this too?" Suruga took out his cell

phone and spoke loud enough for L to hear. "This is Y286."

The man on the other end raised his voice immediately. "What the hell have you been doing, Sugi—Y286? You were supposed to return for debriefing after we took you off the assignment. Then I hear you've been interfering with the recovery team. I assume you recovered the target, since you went renegade on us and are certain to face disciplinary action."

"Yes, the target…" Suruga stared at the Death Note, winked at L, and tossed it to him. "The target…I'm sorry, sir. I couldn't execute the mission."

"What? What are you talking about, Suruga?"

"I can't betray the man who avenged Raye's and Naomi's deaths."

The voice on the end grew irritated. "Suruga, our superiors view L's possession of the Death Note as a serious threat. You'll be dismissed from the Bureau if you continue to collaborate with him. You will be hunted down along with L."

"I understand." Suruga ended the call and smiled.

"Are you all right, Mr. Suruga?" L asked.

"Yeah, we need to worry about Maki first. Besides, working on what will be L's final mission is more exciting. By the way, how did it go?"

"It went well. Our little misdirection was successful in drawing most of the guards away from Professor Nikaido's lab."

†

Once the power was restored inside the Blue Ship hideout, the members flew into a collective uproar.

"Dr. Kujo, we've got trouble! The Death Note—" Konishi said helplessly.

"I know." Kujo held up a hand and turned on the computer, hold-

ing the Chupa Chups L had handed her as a present. She removed the wrapper and found a six-digit number inscribed on the lollipop. Kujo entered the number in the password window for the encrypted microchip they had obtained from L at the Yellow Box warehouse.

"An audio file this time?" Kujo had a bad feeling as she sighed and clicked the mouse. An upbeat song came out of the speakers.

"That voice...Misa Misa?" Konishi said, peeking over Kujo's shoulder. It was a demo of Misa Amane's new single, which L had somehow managed to acquire.

"L, now you've made me angry." Kujo glared at the Chupa Chups like it was L himself. "Konishi, can you still break into the Kira Investigation building's system?"

"Yes, but with everything deleted from the system, it's useless."

"But you can still tap into their outside line. I need you to put your hacking skills to work."

"Huh? Of course..."

Kujo dropped the Chupa Chups on the ground and crushed it with her foot. Konishi's face froze at sight of this unusual display of anger.

"L, people may call you the world's top detective, but what can you do without the authorities to back you?"

L 09-1 Attack

As the dense trees grew sparser, L and Maki rested their tired legs and looked down upon the nightscape of the city below. They had parted ways with Suruga so they could head for their true destination: Osaka. Suruga had taken the truck to have it modified and to obtain a fake license plate.

"We're almost to the rendezvous point," L said. "Suruga should be there already."

"Does this mean we can stop walking these mountain roads?" Maki asked. She lifted a leg. Her sneaker was caked in mud.

"I hope so."

The Pandemic Task Force had initiated a joint inspection with the police and the Ministry of Health, Labour, and Welfare. Inspection teams dressed head to toe in hazmat suits were turning up all across the country. Summer vacation having started, girls resembling Maki were being detained everywhere after being spotted in public libraries, supermarkets, movie theaters, and busy shopping districts by hazmat teams.

L and Maki had chosen the mountain route to evade the inspections. Maki's steps grew lighter as the city lights drew closer from among the trees.

"Right behind the train station. Just a little further—" L stopped suddenly, then tackled Maki to the ground.

"Ryuzaki! What—" A shot rang out.

"One, two...no, four! All armed. And that was not a warning shot." L hid behind a tree and squeezed Maki's hand, signaling her to close her eyes. L lobbed a strobe bomb in the direction of the shots. There was a brilliant flash and the world went white. But this time the enemy wore helmets with tinted visors to counteract the flash.

"Maki, these people are professionals. You need to run. Their aim is to kill me."

"What are you saying? If we run, we run together! Besides, you're the one who said you'd protect me. You said you'd take care of me until the end!" cried Maki. She grabbed L by the shirt and shook him.

L looked at her like he was staring at a talking armadillo. "That selfish act is meant to encourage me, isn't it?"

"You don't have to say it out loud, stupid!"

Another shot glanced off the tree. The two hunkered down even lower. Then fireworks lit up the sky above the city. The sounds of cheering from a distant summer festival drifted in from town.

"We should try to lose them in the festival," L said. "We'll have to make a run for it and zigzag behind the trees."

"Okay!"

The pair broke into a run, enemy fire following at intervals. Once they entered the city, the shooting stopped, but the enemy was still in pursuit. The summer festival was teeming with people.

"Pull your cap down, Maki, so they can't see you."

Gaggles of Gothloli girls in black frilly dresses stood out from among the crowd of people mostly wearing summer yukatas.

"That reminds me..." L said as he recalled the events calendar from Misa Amane's website. Misa's first appearance after a hiatus from the entertainment industry had been scheduled for this summer festival. Finding a program with the pop idol's face on it, Maki said, "Look, it's Misa. It's her comeback tour!" Though she was now known throughout Japan as the pop idol Misa Misa, to Maki, she was still like an older sister from back home. "Ryuzaki, I have an idea!" No sooner had she said it, Maki took L by the hand and dragged him into the event hall. The hall was thronged with fans. Behind the pair, a small group of enemy agents followed. Taking off their helmets, the trackers put on dark sunglasses and gauze masks to guard against the eyes of the shinigami. They kept their distance from L and positioned themselves by the exits.

"They probably won't make a move in this crowd, but we won't be able to escape either."

"Leave that to me! Just wait here," Maki said and moved off toward the stage.

When she returned moments later, Maki flashed the OK sign.

L asked, "What did you do?"

Maki only answered, "Just wait and see."

L shot Maki a disappointed look. But soon he forgot everything when Misa Amane appeared onstage. Enraptured, he began to cheer along with the girls in black lace and frilly skirts. The mini-concert reached a fever pitch when Misa performed for the first time "The Devil's Eye," the follow-up to her first hit single, "Heaven's Door." After the performance, Misa remained onstage to hand out autographed posters, CDs, and T-shirts to the loudest screamers and cutest dressers. She looked out into the crowd with a mischievous smirk and shouted into the mic, "I have to say, I have this thing for sunglasses lately. So for all the guys out there sporting sunglasses, I have a very special present for you! Come on up, guys!"

All eyes turned to the men wearing sunglasses in the crowd. L and Maki's pursuers were of course among them. They quickly started to remove their sunglasses but stopped when they saw L take out a notebook and pencil from under his shirt.

"You there! I see you. Don't be shy, come on up!"

Pressured by both Misa and the gaze of the crowd, a group of brawny men in sunglasses, their features covered in spirit gum and gauze, emerged from the crowd of twelve-year-old girls and shyly took the stage.

"Ryuzaki, now's our chance!" Maki could barely stifle her laughter as she urged L toward the exit.

"You talked to Misa, didn't you. Helpful indeed. But…" L looked back and bit the nail of his forefinger.

"But what?"

"I wanted to win one of those autographed teddy bears," L pouted.

"We don't have time for that! Let's get out of here!"

"Okay." L stopped to look at Misa one more time. "Misa Amane… I hope you enjoy the remaining few years of your life." Then he took Maki by the hand and began to run. But soon, Maki pulled even with him and finally surged forward so she was the pulling L by the hand.

"What, tired already? That's because you're not getting enough nourishment, eating sweets all the time!"

"My brain cells," he said, between gasps, "require…sweets."

The men darted out of the hall with Misa's autographed merchandise in hand and quickly gained ground.

"Now we're in trouble, Ryuzaki!"

As the men drew their guns, dropping posters and dolls and even a pair of plush pillows, a vehicle screeched to a halt in front of their targets. On the side of the truck was a picture of a roasted sweet potato.

"Get in!" Suruga shouted from behind the wheel.

L and Maki climbed in and slammed the door shut. The tinny sound of bullets plunking against the sides of the truck filled the vehicle. But despite its shoddy appearance, the truck, which L called a "mobile operations room," was outfitted with bulletproof windows and special metal plating to withstand the gunfire. The van sped out of the festival's main thoroughfare and toward the isolated warehouse district.

"Thank you, Mr. Suruga," L said.

"Was that FBI?" shouted Suruga. "A little extreme, wouldn't you say?" He spun the wheel hard, sending L and Maki tumbling against the reinforced walls of the truck. He took another sharp turn and cut across three lanes of traffic. "Sorry! Tires aren't bulletproof, so we have to evade!"

"They seem to have changed their tactics. Before, they were after the Death Note, but this time, they just started shooting." Pulling himself into the passenger seat, L began to type away on the laptop and hacked into the FBI system. "It appears you and I have been identified as terrorists threatening the world with the Death Note. FBI agents have been authorized to shoot us on sight."

"Threatening the world! What's that supposed to mean?"

"Apparently the president of the United States received a threat in L's name. Someone must have hacked into the Kira Investigation Headquarters' system and issued the threat as L."

"By someone, you mean…" Suruga remembered Kujo's threat and felt a chill run down his spine.

L did not answer. He continued to nibble on the nails of his fingers.

⅃ 09-2 Purge

The enormous biotope was enshrined, as ever, in the center of Blue Ship's headquarters.

Kujo idly watched the creatures skittering inside the glass as Maki's words swirled inside her head: "I wouldn't be happy living in a peaceful world that was created by sacrificing people's lives."

Are these creatures truly happy? Or are they better off living shorter lives, completely free in the outside world? Kujo shook her head and turned her thoughts back to reality.

"He used decoys to divide our manpower and then broke into this hideout to steal back the Death Note. L…he's not one to be taken lightly," said Matoba, who had been given an account of the night before. He shrugged and let out a quiet sigh. A heavy silence hung over the room as the Blue Ship members ruminated on their failures. Sensing the hit they had taken to their morale, Matoba opted not to rebuke them for their failed efforts. Instead he asked rather genially, "So what now Dr. Kujo? With the Death Note gone, we've lost our best weapon against L."

Kujo nodded and calmly replied, "There's nothing to worry about. Konishi and I have already taken the next step."

"And what might that be?"

"We're going to kill L, and it'll be perfectly legal." There was a buzz of skepticism as the members looked to Kujo. "Konishi hacked into the Kira Investigation Headquarters' system and delivered a threat to the president of the United States posing as L."

"What kind of threat?" asked one of the Blue Shippers, his anxiety obvious in the quiver of his voice.

"Payment of roughly the equivalent of the U.S. national budget. If the president doesn't comply, we threatened to use the Death Note to kill him—after we compel him to pick up the red phone and drop the bomb."

Matoba leaned forward, crossing the other leg. "And what happens then?"

"The president will make it look like he is complying with our demands, but will take covert action to eliminate L. Then with L out of the way, getting our hands on Maki will be easy."

"I see. I am looking forward to seeing how this plays out."

Kujo looked at Matoba's hands. His manicured nails, befitting the man who valued order and unity above everything else, had a look of artificiality. Matoba looked to Kujo like a man of plastic, a bit less than human.

Professor Kagami stood up and gazed at the biotope. "The perfect cycle of nature exists only here in this miniature garden. In order to restore the earth back to the pristine state symbolized by this biotope, half of the world's population must be eliminated. It is precisely the reason I had such high hopes for your proposed global cleansing, this negative population growth plan, with the virus, Mr. Matoba."

"I'm well aware, Professor Kagami."

Kagami directed a stern gaze at Matoba's back. "Then why are you seeking a buyer for the virus?"

"I beg your pardon?"

"Don't play dumb with me. The European Union, the American establishment, Russia, the Middle East. You have been weighing their bids."

Matoba smiled the serene smile members of Blue Ship had seen many times before. "I would never do something so disgraceful," he said. "I am merely looking for a group to establish a long-term partnership with. As you know, the virus must be scattered simultaneously in key areas. To enable that, we need to become partners with an entity who has resources sufficient to distribute the virus across the ecosystem. We need someone with a global network." Matoba's peaceful demeanor remained unchanged.

Kagami knew full well that this was the horrifying aspect of Matoba's personality. But he could no longer idly stand by and watch the goals of the group being derailed. "Is that how you plan to drive up the selling price of the virus? You want the antidote data, not for our cause, but so you can increase the virus's value. In the end, you're only after money and power. Don't you understand that this very kind of greed and self-interest is what brought the world to the brink of total oblivion? That is what we are trying to stop!"

Matoba let out a sigh and gestured to Hatsune with a look. Hatsune approached Kagami. "Why, you look a little tired, Professor Kagami," she said as she rested a hand on the professor's shoulder. "Maybe you'd like to take a nap—" Then her stiletto sank into the man's heart. For a moment, Kagami stared at Hatsune with a bewildered look. He didn't even have the chance to feel pain. Looking down, he realized that the knife had been plunged inside his body to the hilt. Hatsune twisted the blade, filling Kagami's heart with air, then pulled it out. His eyes rolled to the back of his head. Kagami crumpled to the ground. Hatsune didn't have a drop of his blood on her.

Hatsune bent down next to the body and closed its eyes. "Have a good sleep," she said. The blood welled up and spread out around the body in gradual ripples, perhaps in time to a heart that no longer pumped.

Matoba looked down at Kagami's body from the sofa where he sat, stone-faced. "Unavoidable, I'm afraid. I'm sure it was apparent to all of you that the old man was beginning to doubt our plan. One person's doubt will spread through the group like a virus and eventually lead to its collapse."

Inwardly Matoba had to gloat over Kagami's timely death. With morale low as a result of L countering their plans, the group was in dire need of either some positive or negative reinforcement. To that end, Professor Kagami had become a sacrifice. Negative reinforcement it was.

The Blue Ship members looked down at the dead body, stares vacant, faces numb. This was the third purge since Matoba had joined the group and radicalized their activities. Without a word, two of the stronger-looking men took hold of Kagami's ankles and wrists and dragged his body to the biotope, and flung it in, as usual. Ravenous eels swarmed the body at once.

†

When Kujo returned home, the phone rang. She picked it up and spoke to her caller in English. "If you're calling, it must mean that you got out. Yesterday? Just in the nick of time. Can you come to Japan right away? You're wanted? Okay, what's the alias?" Her tone was friendly as she let out a carefree laugh.

"Can I hold them off until you arrive? Don't worry. Matoba has yet to get his hands on it. The elusive detective is prolonging the chase." The calculating smile of a woman with a secret came over her face. "L has managed to keep them guessing, as might have been expected. Worthy of the title of world's top detective, yes," she said, sarcasm coloring the words. "You and I can work together again, thanks to him. Now's our time to move ahead with our plan. Don't worry, the plan is fail proof. Yes, I'll see you when you get here. I'm going to destroy this phone now, so you'll receive the new number through the usual method. Right, bye."

Kujo deleted the call history before putting down the phone. Then she opened the desk drawer, removed the false bottom, and produced two photographs from the hidden compartment. One faded picture showed her parents smiling over Kujo as a young girl as she blew out the candles of a birthday cake. It was the last picture they had taken together as a family.

Suddenly one image came back to her: her younger self, standing helplessly before a burning building.

"Mom, Dad, it took some time, but we're nearly there..." There was a childlike innocence in Kujo's face as she spoke to the image of her parents suspended in time. Then she stopped to look at the man in the other photograph. He had been an indispensable presence, who supported her and believed in her when she had lost the will to live after losing her parents. She recalled what he had said to her in parting:

—*Keep your way.*

Though she tried to forget the words, they only echoed louder the more she tried to lock them away. The words conveyed the man's recognition of her ability to change the world as well as the man's trust in her to use her abilities *to* change the world. "Please understand, Watari. This is the only way I believe…I can change the world," she said, as much to convince herself.

The entryway's security alarm went off. Hastily, she put away the photographs and checked to see if there were anything suspicious lying around. Then she waited for the doorbell to ring before she answered the door.

"Konishi. What are you doing here so late?" Detecting the effect the purge had on Konishi in his helpless face, Kujo let him inside. Sitting him down in a chair, Kujo tried to calm him down. She could not afford to lose such a useful pawn now.

"Am I really going to be…safe?" Konishi had his head down and appeared more nervous than usual.

She reached across the table and took his hand. "Konishi, do you think there's any future in being a lackey for Matoba and Yoshizawa? Neither values you as person. They're only using you for your programming and hacking skills, you know that. I don't want to have to tell you this, but once this plan succeeds, I guarantee you, Matoba will toss you out on the street."

"I know, but I'm terrified that I'll end up like Professor Kagami." Konishi was more traumatized than Kujo had imagined. Kujo stood up and went to his side. Konishi buried his face in her chest like a child.

"It's all right. Leave everything to me. You don't have a thing to worry about." She cradled him in her bosom and stroked his hair. There was not even a shadow of a smile on Kujo's face.

𝕃07-1 Escape

The sweet potato truck traveled up a mountain road that could hardly be called a road at all. Occasionally Suruga jumped out of the truck to move a rock or fallen tree that blocked the path before resuming the slow crawl up the mountain.

"Are you sure this is the only road we can take?" The blue signs peeking out timidly from the overgrown ivy displayed a three-digit number, which indicated that this unpaved road was a national highway. "This isn't a national highway, it's a highway to hell," Suruga muttered.

Without paying Suruga any mind, the woman in the passenger seat accessed the system of an area police department. The GPS onscreen showed the road map as well as the inspection checkpoints in red. "Routes 19, 21, 65, 402 all have checkpoints. This road will end in seven kilometers. Keep going, honey."

"Will you stop it with the honeys? You're giving me the creeps," Suruga snapped, a chill shooting up his spine. L smiled at him, his lips glossy with lipstick and a flattering female wig on his head. Maki was disguised as a boy thanks to a Hanshin Tigers cap. The three had managed to clear the checkpoints posing as a family.

"You don't have to be embarrassed." L's face was serious as he winked at Suruga. Suruga felt another chill and shivered.

Maki laughed. "This feels like a real family. We used to go out driving in a small, beat-up car like this when my mom was still alive."

"This truck may be small but it's not beat-up," L said, petulant.

Maki looked down and teared up. She began to cry on L's shoulder. L went stiff as a rod.

"I may call myself the world's top detective, but I haven't a clue what to do in this case." He reached out with a hand and patted Maki's head a little too roughly. Maki was still, even as she scrunched her face as L seemed to massage her head more than stroke it.

"Ryuzaki, there's no way we'll make our destination at this pace."

"I know. Wait another two hours."

"Two hours?"

"Yes, I have a plan. Until then, keep going, honey," L said suggestively. He reapplied some lipstick and winked at Suruga again.

†

The sound of crickets filled the air. L and Maki lay on their backs gazing upward. A star-filled sky spread out before them.

"They're so beautiful. I never thought about stars before, but now that I know I'm dying, they really are beautiful." Wiping away a tear, Maki reached up with both arms toward the stars, which looked close enough to touch.

"I didn't think I was equipped to feel an emotion so imperfect and passive, but right now, I am touched by the sight of these stars."

L and Maki continued to look up at the luminous stars they might never see again.

"Say Ryuzaki, were you ever able to catch Kira?"

"No, while I was able to stop the killing, I was unable to catch him."

"Why not?"

"Kira died."

"Then I guess you lost."

"Why do you say that?" L sat up abruptly at the mention of defeat. But when she stared back at him, he scratched his head.

"He died a bad man, right? Your job is to catch him so you can make him see that what he did was a bad thing. If you couldn't do either, that means you lost."

"You're right," L said after a long moment of thought. "I lost."

"Not even close to winning."

"No, not even close," L said in a rare admission of defeat. He lay down again to contemplate the stars. He wrapped a hand protectively around the watch on his wrist.

"What are you thinking about, Ryuzaki?"

"I was thinking about my only friend."

"Did that broken watch belong to him?"

"Yes." Maki's hand reached out and rested on top of L's. For a moment, L remained awkwardly still. Then he asked, "Maki...should I hold your hand in this case?"

"Ryuzaki, in this case, you should shut up and hold it real tight."

"All right." He gave a satisfied nod and squeezed Maki's hand.

Maki's body shook from laughing. "You really don't know anything, do you, Ryuzaki?"

"That's the first time anyone has told me that."

The two laughed like brother and sister.

"How about you two stop fooling around and help me for a change? There's no telling when they're going to come after us again." Suruga peeked out from under the truck, brandishing a wrench. His face was blackened with grease. "Maybe I can squeeze a few more miles out of this truck, but I doubt it."

"It's nearly time." L sat up mechanically and pulled out a cell phone. It was the only hotline he had taken with him from the Kira Investigation Headquarters. The words "President of the United

States" were scribbled on the back of it in L's handwriting.

"Mr. President? This is L," he said casually, as though talking to a friend. Then L declared, "You don't seem to be taking my threat seriously. Ten minutes from now, I will commit a murder using the Death Note. The victim will be the mob boss Rod Ross, currently incarcerated in Arizona State Penitentiary."

L ended the call and opened the Death Note. Holding the pencil precariously by the end, L wrote down the name:

—*Rod Ross*

will die of a heart attack July 23, 22:30.

"What's going on, Ryuzaki? You said you wouldn't use the Death Note." Suruga had never before objected to L's plans no matter how eccentric they seemed, because he had believed L was only thinking ahead, and in truth, everything had gone according to plan thus far. This time, however, he could only believe that L was acting out of desperation.

However, L ignored him entirely and closed notebook. "Mr. Suruga, would you mind making us some coffee?" Ten minutes later, after L had gulped down coffee sweetened beyond measure, he picked up the phone again.

"So what do you say, Mr. President? Do you see now that I am being serious?" There was a murmur on the other end of the line. "Then please consider our demand of ten billion dollars. And let me remind you that I am capable of writing, 'The President of the United States, David Hope, will die after launching nuclear missiles at London, Moscow, and Beijing.' If I am attacked in any way, I will assume that you gave the order and write your name in the Death Note."

L 07-2 Multiple

A heavy silence hung over the Oval Office. The vice president and cabinet secretaries gathered around the beleaguered president. They exchanged distressed looks, but little else. Finally, Vice President Godwin had no choice but to break the silence. "The Death Note has proven to be authentic. If the next contingency fails, L will use the notebook to assassinate the president for certain. I recommend using a small tactical nuclear weapon. L must be eliminated."

"But to use a nuclear weapon against a friendly nation…The people of Japan are especially sensitive to the use of nuclear arms," said the secretary of state, a woman named Beal. "A tactical strike could lead to an all-out nuclear war just as surely as the Death Note threat."

President Hope tapped his fingers against the desk, as was his habit when deep in thought. The tapping echoed in the room as it also ticked off the passage of time.

Finally the tapping stopped. Hope looked up and said, "We have no alternative. We'll use a tack nuke. We'll say we were targeting Kira. L has already killed with the Death Note—he *is* the new Kira."

The mention of a new Kira brought everyone to a consensus. When the president moved to put in a call to the army's Special Forces, the red light on the hotline lit up again.

"What is this? It's from L again." Caught off guard, the president hit the speaker button. "What do you want, L? I told you that I needed more time to—"

"Mr. President, this is a different L from the L who has been threatening you."

"A different L…What do you mean?" The president looked to the others for an answer. The cabinet members assembled could only shake their heads and listen in on the conversation.

"Mr. President, you must be aware that L is not a single person

126

but an investigative group comprised of multiple Ls."

"Y-yes."

The amorphous Detective L. The rumors, speculation, and hypotheses about L's identity were endless. One rumor proposed that it was the alias of the great detective Lloyd F. Scope, who had purportedly disappeared back in the '70s and died. (Although, were he alive today, he would be well over a hundred.) Then there was another rumor that the world's top three detectives, L, Eraldo Coil, and Danuve, were one and the same. And the most credible rumor, which the intelligence agencies sought to verify, was that L was not one person but an investigative group comprised of multiple Ls.

Ever since the emergence of L's name in society, the difficult and mysterious cases that he (or she) had solved were countless and far exceeded the number of arrests made by any one investigative bureau. That one person could crack so many high-profile cases was inconceivable. But not once had L made any definitive statement about whether L was an individual or a group until now.

"Let's say we call the person threatening you L-Prime. With his possession and use of the Death Note, L-Prime has broken from our investigative group and signaled his revolt against us." L's electronically altered voice resonated in the Oval Office. "This investigative unit will not forgive this betrayal. L-Prime's actions have profaned the L name and contradicts our mission. Leave L-Prime to us. We will bring this matter to a conclusion within one week. We will stake our reputation on it."

"All right, let me consider it." The president hung up the phone and began tapping on the desk again. Then he turned to the people in the room and said, "No tactical nuclear weapons."

"Mr. President?" the others shouted at once.

"I'm not entirely convinced by the call. But as long as there is the slightest possibility that there is more than one L, we have to realize that we might end up going against all of them."

The vice president nodded. "Agreed. As long as we don't act first, L won't write the president's name in the Death Note. The best strategy for now is to wait a week, while putting off L-Prime's demand."

The president picked up the phone and was patched through to the director of the FBI. "Inform your agents on the L case that there has been a change in plans. Suspend the operation to eliminate L but continue to monitor his activities covertly. And eliminate anyone who tries to harm him."

L 07-3 Flight

"Now onto the next phase of our plan." L brought up meteorological data on the laptop and fumbled around in the truck for a long tarp. "It's my hot air balloon," he explained in the most bare-bones way.

So this was all a part of his plan too...Suruga watched L quickly put together a burner and assemble a black plastic gondola. The balloon had been delivered to Suruga while he was having the truck modified, and he had simply loaded the cargo into the truck without noting its sender or contents.

"The wind will shift west around midnight. We'll fly as close to Osaka as we can."

"I see; we'll be virtually undetectable flying in the dark. And by air, there won't be any fallen trees to worry about."

Suruga started to climb into the gondola when L stopped him. "Mr. Suruga, this balloon is for two."

"You want me to stay behind?"

"Yes, we'll need the truck once we arrive in Osaka. You'll need

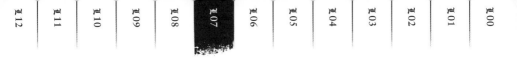

to repair it and get it to Osaka somehow. You'll have to modify it again, since the inspection checkpoints are on the lookout for a sweet potato truck."

Slowly the burner filled the envelope with hot air and the balloon began to take shape.

"By the way, Mr. Suruga, you have a class two boat license, do you not?"

"Yeah, but you probably knew that when you checked out my history. What, is there going to be a boat after the balloon?"

"Yes, it is a possibility."

Now what, Suruga thought to himself, but he no longer felt the need to ask. L would tell him, of course, but Suruga now felt that asking him would spoil the surprise.

The balloon began to lift softly off the ground. L hopped into the gondola and then, with arms outstretched, collected Maki and placed her next to him.

"See you in Osaka, Ryuzaki! Take care, Maki!"

"Take care, Mr. Suruga!" Maki shouted.

Gradually the black balloon ascended and made its way under the cover of darkness. As it gained altitude, the balloon caught a westward breeze. A sea of city lights spread out below. The orderly street lights, the blinking traffic signals, the lamps illuminating the home windows...To Maki, they all seemed to flicker like the crystallizations of people's hopes and dreams. "Isn't it pretty, Ryuzaki?" She thought of all the beautiful lights and what remained of her short life, and she began to tear up.

L did not hesitate to take her hand this time, and he held it tightly. "There is happiness in each and every one of those lights. I won't allow anyone to shatter them."

𝕃 06-1 Arrival

It was early morning, and the rattle of a cart echoed down the streets of Osaka. Out of the morning fog emerged a rickshaw, pulled by L in yet another costume. Maki rode in the chair. L said breathlessly, "Kyoto to Osaka...was too far..."

"That's because you steered the balloon the wrong way!"

"But thanks to my error, we were able to eat *yatsuhashi* in Kyoto. By the way, Maki, I realize I already asked but—"

"That again? No way! This cell phone is a keepsake from my mom, and I'm not throwing it away."

"Oh. That's too bad." L scanned the area for suspicious activity as he ran. A car was trailing their rickshaw. Their shortcut by hot air balloon had probably been picked up by satellite. "Leave it to the FBI. They've already tracked down our location."

"Did you say something, Ryuzaki?"

"Just talking to myself."

L mustered the last of his strength and pulled the rickshaw even faster.

†

"What do you mean by dragging a girl infected with a deadly

virus around in public, you idiot! What if she had begun to exhibit symptoms?" Takahashi nearly blew L back out the door of the lab with his yelling.

Although Takahashi was now retired, he was once a prominent immunologist who vied with Nikaido for the top spot in their field. L scratched his head meekly, not having had much experience with being scolded.

Maki was in the bathroom taking a shower. Since they hadn't had the opportunity to bathe on the run, it was the first time Maki felt refreshed in a long while.

"Maki, I'm putting all of your dirty clothes in the wash. I'll leave you a change of clothes here." Hitomi, Takahashi's wife, called to her from outside the door.

"Yes, thank you."

Enveloped by the warmth of the shower, Maki felt contented. Something about Hitomi reminded her of her own mother. As she scrubbed herself with a washcloth, Maki looked at her arm and froze. The sound of the shower filled the room as if to wash away any feeling of happiness she'd just felt.

A rash had appeared on her arm.

Maki's face was ashen when she returned from showering.

"What's wrong, Maki?" L noticed the change almost immediately.

"Professor Takahashi. Quarantine me."

"The symptoms...?" Takahashi rushed to Maki's side and pulled her arm closer to him. He examined the two spots on her arm and shot L a stern look.

"She has the symptoms, doesn't she?" L asked.

Looking at their worried faces, Takahashi grinned and patted Maki on the head. "It's just a tick bite. From your escape through the mountains." Maki stood there blankly for a moment, then sank down helplessly on the tatami floor, breathing a sigh of relief. "Let that be a lesson to you. There is no predicting the onset of the virus. Two weeks is only an average. The actual onset depends on many factors, such as the carrier's general health and stress level."

Takahashi turned back to the composition of the antidote from the data Professor Nikaido had left behind. "I see, so what Nikaido managed to discover was a completely new type of interferon," he said between bites of the *yatsuhashi* L had brought as a gift. These red bean-filled snacks disappeared one by one as if Takahashi might eat the entire box himself. L stared enviously, finger in his mouth.

Gathering himself, L asked, "Professor Takahashi, I'm afraid I only have a layman's knowledge of immunology. Will you explain it to me?"

"Of course. First you must know that the human body is very sophisticated and has various defense mechanisms against foreign bodies entering the system."

"Such as running a fever when you get the flu, correct?"

"Right, most people tend to think that the influenza virus is the cause of the fever, but in reality, it is an immune response to try to inhibit viral replication...*Hrgh!*..in the body. W-wait." Takahashi pounded his chest to try to dislodge the gooey yatsuhashi clogging his throat and gulped down his tea in panic. "Phew, almost choked there. That was an immune response to inhibit the *yatsuhashi* virus from replicating."

"Huh?"

"That was a joke."

"I'm not good with jokes."

"Right. Well anyway, while a fever or inflammation are readily recognizable immune responses, there are many other ways that the immune system protects the body. For example, macrophages ingest virus cells and help destroy them, while a type of white blood cell called neutrophils works to dissolve foreign agents inside the body. One substance, which is critical to fighting viruses, is a protein called interferons. How much do you know about interferons?"

Maki raised her hand like she was in class. "It's a drug used to treat Hepatitis C!"

"Correct! It's famous as a drug for treating Hepatitis C and tumors. Interferons are proteins that are secreted to surrounding cells as foreign agents enter the body. Once the proteins are produced, they act on the host cells surrounding the virus cells to make them virus-resistant, thereby inhibiting viral replication. If interferons could be made to work effectively inside the body, even virulent viruses such as Ebola would no longer be a threat."

"So you're saying interferons do not work against hemorrhagic fevers like the Ebola virus."

"That's right. Hemorrhagic fever viruses block the function of interferons. That's why Nikaido's new interferon is so helpful."

"You inject the host with the professor's new interferon, which the hemorrhagic fever virus can't block, thereby helping the host cells become virus-resistant," L said.

"Does that mean I'm cured?" Maki looked at L hopefully. L took Maki's hand and gave it a reassuring squeeze.

"Evidently Nikaido found an uninfected chimpanzee at the outbreak site in the remote Congo. It's been said that non-human interferons are typically less effective in humans, but...By the way, you're going to need white blood cells from a chimp according to Nikaido's data."

"Not to worry. We have it right here." L took out the small vial he had brought with him from Tokyo. "We took the scenic route so that I could sneak into Nikaido's lab and extract a sample of the chimp's blood."

"You cultivate enough of these cells and synthesize them with the virus cells extracted from Maki's blood, the cells will become infected with the virus and begin to produce interferons. Refine that and you have the antidote."

"Will it be possible to make it in time?" L asked.

Takahashi studied the calendar on the wall. "It's been a week since infection, which means you'd have to get started right away."

"Yes. However, the Pandemic Task Force has already been compromised—a terrorist is working in their midst. Which is why, Professor Takahashi, I'd like you to produce the antidote."

"Now wait a minute, you're asking me to produce the antidote?" Takahashi's mood changed completely. He answered, "I can't."

"Professor Nikaido could, though. You two were partners once." L held up a book taken from Watari's library entitled *Infectious Disease Research*, co-authored by Nikaido and Takahashi.

"Years ago, a vaccine I developed...failed. Profound negative side effects." Takahashi looked down and shook his head. "I killed people. I promised myself never again."

"No doubt there were many victims from that incident. But so many others have been saved by your research. Only you can save Maki's life."

Takahashi let out a deep sigh. A long forgotten memory seemed to creep up on him, but he hastily shook it off. He looked at Maki, who stood tall, trying not to look afraid.

Hitomi, who had been listening quietly, put a gentle hand on her husband's shoulder. "Do it for them."

"Hitomi..."

"Professor Nikaido would have wanted you to try to save his daughter."

After a long silence, Takahashi stood and put a hand on Maki's head. "All right. Looks like I'm the one to do it."

"Thank you," Maki said. L and Maki bowed at the same time.

"But producing the antidote requires extracting the virus from Maki's blood. The risk of infection will be high. Plus, this place isn't equipped to handle level four viruses. The best I have is a biological safety cabinet, which isn't completely airtight. Maybe we should look for a research facility we can use?"

L shook his head. "It's highly likely the terrorist group is keeping an eye on the research facilities in the country, waiting for us to begin work on the antidote."

"Are you telling me I not only need to synthesize the antidote myself, but that I have to put all our lives in jeopardy to do it?"

"It will be fine," L said. "All you need to do is succeed in producing the antidote before you begin to exhibit symptoms."

"A dangerous gamble. No matter how completely we seal off this lab, it just isn't possible to absolutely prevent the virus from infecting one of us. If even one person is infected in this densely populated area, the virus will spread very quickly. If that happens, a research facility of this scale won't be able to manufacture the necessary amount of the antidote in time."

L was staring off in an unexpected direction. The object of his attention was a photograph of Takahashi proudly holding up a twenty-inch red seabream on a long-ago fishing trip.

L 06-2 Discovery

"Can't you find them yet?" Matoba snapped. Two days had passed since the information on the girl stopped coming in, and Matoba was beginning to show his impatience.

"We checked all of the labs and research facilities L might go to with the virus, but we came up empty," said one Blue Ship member. He gestured with the reports he held in his hand and shrugged.

"After they were spotted in the mountains in Yamanashi Prefecture, nothing from the checkpoints...At this point, they could only have flown," Konishi said. If L were listening he might have said,

"Well done."

"You've been talking big about how you would kill L, Dr. Kujo, but no word yet."

Matoba shot an icy glare at Kujo, who stood petrified.

She had periodically continued to hack into the Kira Investigation Headquarters' line to send threats to the president. However, the president had shown no sign of moving against L. Since the Death Note was not actually in her possession, Kujo couldn't follow through on her threats or even demonstrate the power she claimed to have.

Matoba, who sat on the sofa in front of the biotope, restlessly crossed his legs again. In order to drive up the selling price of the virus, the virus had to be effectively spread across the country to demonstrate the widespread damage it could cause. Maki could not be allowed to spread the virus first in a haphazard way.

"The GPS on the girl's cell phone still isn't—hey!" Konishi switched screens and shouted, "What's going on? There's only one GPS signal."

The members gathered around.

"The dummy transmitters probably went dead."

"Then this signal is the girl's location."

"She's in Osaka," Kujo said.

The Blue Ship gang stood as one.

𝕃06-3 Production

"I always dreamed of fishing on a cruiser, but I never thought I'd be using one for this," said Takahashi. He looked out at sea with his arms crossed. When he turned around, however, he was brought back to reality. The main cabin of the luxury yacht, which would

136

normally be occupied by a lavish sofa set, was filled with laboratory equipment from Takahashi's lab.

"A change in thinking. If we can't completely contain the virus, then we need only go to a place where no damage would be done if the virus did escape quarantine. When the production of the antidote is finished, the cruiser is yours, Professor Takahashi."

"Idiot. This thing is bigger than my house! I can't even afford to maintain it!"

"Spoken like a true Osakan," L said, apparently as a compliment.

L climbed up the stairs to the wheelhouse. "Mr. Suruga, how are you doing navigating the boat?"

Suruga took off his sunglasses and shrugged. He had left the repairs on the truck to an underground shop in Nagoya and arrived in Osaka a step ahead of L and Maki. "I've finally regained the feel for it. But Ryuzaki, will we really be able to contain the spread of the virus out at sea?"

"We can't be 100 percent certain, but the powerful summer ultraviolet rays will destroy most of the virus that might get carried out to sea by the wind."

"Couldn't the marine life get infected and in turn infect humans?"

"Hemorrhagic fever viruses are airborne and settle in respiratory tissue. Fish don't have lungs."

"Then, could a whale or dolphin get infected?"

"If so, you can present them at the next research conference as the first marine mammals to be infected with a hemorrhagic fever virus."

After listening quietly to this exchange, Takahashi threw a couple of hazmat suits at them. "Quit your comedy routine and change into these suits so you can make yourselves useful. Ryuzaki will be my assistant and Suruga will navigate the cruiser. And try not to rock the boat when we're handling syringes."

"Aye aye!" Putting on his sunglasses again, Suruga surveyed the open water. About a kilometer off was another vessel. With four anchor chains descending from the bow, it was neither a fishing boat nor pleasure boat, and was obviously watching over the cruiser. "So they've come all the way out here. L must have put the fear of God into the president. Blue Ship ought to be closer to tracking us by now, but we can rest easy knowing the FBI is here. But who would have thought the FBI would be the ones to protect us…That's a fine irony."

L 05   Pirates

Two boats cruised the calm waters of Osaka Bay under the cover of night. As they headed for the light of the cruiser ahead, Kujo, a passenger on the lead ship, murmured, "How clever of you to think of the open sea, L. There's little threat of the virus spreading here."

Yoshizawa, binoculars in hand, spoke to the members aboard both vessels over a transceiver. "The girl is aboard the cruiser. We'll split up and attack from both sides in five minutes. We need to take them before L has the chance to use the Death Note." Yoshizawa saw the men on the deck aboard the boat cruising alongside them nod. "Unlike the warehouse, there's nowhere to escape this time."

A third ship altered course, churning up a huge wake as it cut across the sea lanes and blocked the Blue Ship vessels' course toward the cruiser. Before anyone could understand what was happening, the interceptor flooded the decks of the ships with blinding white light.

The interceptor's crew wore no military uniforms, but rather sunglasses and gauze masks. With a minimum of movement, the boat had succeeded in containing the two Blue Ship vessels and prevented them from getting any closer to the cruiser.

"These bastards are pros. Dammit! We can't get any closer!" Yoshizawa said over the radio.

Kujo threw an arm over her eyes and squinted carefully. "Sunglasses and masks...to guard against the Death Note. The FBI is protecting L," Kujo said, astonished.

"What's happening, Kujo? I thought you manipulated the FBI into killing L."

"L...just what kind of spell did you cast?" Kujo had no way to learn the reason for the FBI's change of heart, of course. While it was still possible to hack into the Kira Investigation Headquarters' system, it would certainly seem odd if Kujo, who was threatening the president posing as L, asked him why the U.S. hadn't moved to kill L.

"What do we do, Kujo? We can't go back and face Matoba after this."

Kujo stared past the interceptor and toward the yacht. Its proximity was tantalizing, but there was no way for the Blue Ship vessels to reach it. Kujo could only bite her lip...and contemplate her next step.

Aboard the cruiser, L and Maki were watching television, unaware of the excitement only a few knots away. The Tigers were playing the rival Giants. Maki, wearing a Tigers' cap and with a plastic megaphone in hand, yelled and screamed at every move the players made. Contrary to the warmth with which Hitomi looked on, L, who also wore a Tigers' cap, observed Maki curiously.

"Get a hit! A homerun every at-bat!"

"This player's batting average is .251, so the odds of his hitting a homerun every at-bat is about once every five thousand games."

"I know that!" Maki shot him a discouraged look. "But you're supposed to cheer loudest for the underdogs. That's what die-hard fans do! Oh, how I'd love an autographed ball!"

"You really love this team."

"Of course! There isn't anyone in Osaka who doesn't love the Tigers."

After watching Maki go on excitedly about the game, L turned his attention on the computer and stuck a *manju* in his mouth.

ℒ04 **Bug**

"In Osaka, you ought to fit right in," Suruga said to the newly painted truck in a warehouse on the docks. "You've been through a lot." The bright red mobile operations room had been painted to look like a *takoyaki* truck. The cartoon octopus on the side represented the local fried delicacy. Suruga patted the cartoon. "Tentacular!"

As Suruga drove back to the pier at which he was to rendezvous with the cruiser, he noticed a suspicious-looking car. Judging from how the car was parked—its front pointed away from the water and hidden in the shadow of a warehouse—Suruga guessed that it didn't belong to a couple of dating kids or to some local fisherman. Then, as if on cue, a man emerged from the car to do some stretching exercises.

"That's—" Suruga recognized the man as a member of Blue Ship. Disgusted by the man's total lack of caution, Suruga idled the truck, casually walked out, and then snuck up to the man from behind and grabbed him in a full nelson.

"An amateur like yourself shouldn't be entrusted to do surveillance work, especially against the FBI. Trying to plant a bug aboard the cruiser?"

The man said nothing. He struggled to writhe free, but Suruga had locked in the hold and had begun to press down on the man's neck.

"Now then, Sonny. Tell me your name. Your full name." The man grunted and did not answer. "Nah, I guess you wouldn't tell me since we have the Death Note. But…"

Suruga swung the man against the hood of the car, then released one of his arms, retaining a half nelson and pinning the Blue Ship man against the car with his weight. Suruga pulled a penknife from his breast pocket and thrust it inside the man's mouth. The man went stiff.

"Ever feel the kind of pain that makes you want to die?" Suruga jabbed the inside of the man's cheek with the point of the knife, stretching the soft flesh till it tented out, the blade's tip straining against the inside of the cheek. The man's eyes opened wide in terror. Suruga loosened his grip, sensing that his captive had been easily broken.

"T-Tatsuhiko…Nakanishi."

"Nakanishi, is it?" Suruga slid the bag on the passenger seat closer to him and dumped its contents on the hood of the car. The man's driver's license fell out.

"Tha-that's…"

Relishing the man's dismayed look, Suruga glanced down at the license. "It says here 'Tatsuya Ohnishi.' Since when did we start reading that as 'Nakanishi' in Japan?" Suruga waved the license in front of him, and the man dropped his head in defeat. "All right, Ohnishi. I have a favor to ask. You do as I say and you won't have to die."

"What do you want?"

Suruga replied, "It's simple really."

†

"Dr. Kujo, all of your plans have failed miserably. How do you plan to take responsibility?" Matoba asked in his most polite yet condescending voice. L, Suruga, Takahashi, and Maki listened in on

the phone conversation, though it was occasionally muffled by static. Holding the teddy bear in her arms, Maki cringed at the sound of the man's mocking voice.

"That Ohnishi fellow sure did us a favor," Suruga said a little proudly. "The bug he planted at the Blue Ship headquarters is working perfectly. Well, almost."

There was a long silence on the other end of the receiver. Finally Kujo said calmly, "I understand. I will carry out the virus plan myself. Please take refuge somewhere overseas."

"But if the antidote isn't finished, you will die," Matoba said.

There were murmurs in the background, some of the members expressing concern.

"No, I am responsible for my repeated failures; I underestimated L. Allow me to do it." Kujo's voice was unwavering.

"If you feel that strongly about it, we have no choice. We will proceed with the plan. I assure you, Dr. Kujo, we will bring this plan to fruition, so your sacrifice will not be in vain."

"This Matoba guy sickens me. He gives Kujo no way out and then talks like she was the one who made the decision." Suruga spat in disgust.

L had been listening to the conversation as he stared at the *butaman*, Osaka's own regional variation on the pork bun, in his hand like he was appraising an antique. "According to the conversation, it appears their aim is to wipe out Japan with the virus."

"Unleashing the virus. What an atrocity." Takahashi let out a heavy sigh.

"But none of them seems to know that Kujo was infected when Maki injected her with the virus," Suruga pointed out.

"Dr. Kujo seems to be hiding that fact from them for some reason. About the conversation just now…" After taking a bite out of the pork-filled bun, L frowned as if something were missing. Breaking the bun in half, he poured maple syrup over the pork-filled center.

While Suruga and Maki, who were used to L's eating habits by now, managed to look away, Takahashi grabbed his chest as if struck with a sudden case of heartburn. L continued, "I believe we were meant to hear this conversation."

"Meant to hear—why do you think that?" Suruga questioned. He declined, or rather rejected, the bun L held out for him.

"I don't believe that Blue Ship would move ahead with the plan without the antidote in their hands. If that were the case, they would have released the virus soon after they attacked the research lab. I believe this conversation was designed to rattle us by announcing their impending plans."

"Do you mean to tell me that Ohnishi got caught intentionally? That's not how it looked to me."

"Yeah, but if it's true, then Dr. Kujo..." Maki let out anxiously.

"Maki, Dr. Kujo is the one who betrayed you and killed your father," L said.

"I know that. But..." Maki's somber face did not change despite L's repeated offerings of pork-filled buns.

L02-1 Kidnapped

With the antidote complete, the cruiser docked at the edge of the pier so Suruga could go buy some groceries in town. Aboard the cruiser, L and Takahashi feasted on skewers of *kushikatsu*, another Osaka specialty Hitomi had made, and although it was not yet evening, a modest celebration had begun.

"Tomorrow I'll run some tests and inoculate Maki. After that, we inform the police about the terrorists' plan, clear Nikaido's name, and it's done."

"Indeed. As for how to pass the antidote on to Dr. K, who's been infected as well…Well, I suppose there would be any number of ways once she is in police custody." L took a bite from the skewer of fried pork and dunked it back in the sauce.

"Hey! Ryuzaki, no double-dipping!" Takahashi scolded.

"Really?"

"The sauce is for everybody, so you can't dip something you already put your mouth on. Double-dipping is strictly prohibited."

"No need to worry." L reached for a container of sauce with the words RYUZAKI'S PERSONAL SAUCE on the side.

"You're prepared." Takahashi looked at L's sauce. "Say, do you mind if I try some of that sauce?"

Without a word, L held out the container for Takahashi. The

professor allowed the sauce to seep in and took a bite of the meat. His eyes spun as a taste he'd never experienced before spread inside his mouth. Unable to spit it out, he gulped the terrible concoction down.

"S-sweet. Ryuzaki, this isn't...?"

"Chocolate sauce. No double-dipping allowed."

"Nobody would double-dip in that thing, idiot." As Takahashi wiped his mouth repeatedly with tissues, Hitomi came in with more prepared dishes. "Isn't Maki eating?"

"She said she wasn't feeling very well. I'll go check on her. By the way, did you talk to Mr. Ryuzaki?"

"Yes, that's right." After finally washing down the sweetness of the chocolate with beer, Takahashi leaned forward in his chair. "Listen, Ryuzaki, Hitomi and I were talking about how Maki is all alone now, having lost both her parents, and we were thinking about adopting her as our daughter. What do you think?"

L smiled. "Thank you. Now I can—"

"You can what?"

"Nothing." Despite having only two days left to live, L lifted his glass. "Professor Takahashi, let us make a toast."

"Right. To the completion of the antidote and to Maki's happiness."

Just as they were about to clink their glasses, Hitomi returned. "Maki is gone!"

L and Takahashi rushed into Maki's cabin to find a chocolate bar and letter on the table. The letter was addressed to L.

—*Dear Ryuzaki,*

Thanks for everything. I thought about it, and I decided to do what I have to do after all.

"What is it that she has to do?" Takahashi asked after stealing a peek at the letter.

L thought for a moment then turned on the computer inside the cabin. He pulled up the most recent search history on the Internet, and a weather map of Osaka popped up.

"A weather map? So she was looking at this before she ran away. Was she worried about rain?"

"No, she was checking the wind direction." L bit his nails more violently than usual.

"Wind direction," Takahasi repeated. "That could be dangerous."

†

Ships crisscrossed the calm waters of Osaka Bay.

Maki took off the Tigers cap and looked at the promontory where she and her parents used to visit with the Amane family when they lived in Osaka. She stood at the edge of the cliff and turned her back on the water. The wind blew directly at her face and outward toward the bay.

"This should be safe, right, Daddy?"

Several moments later, a lone figure arrived and approached Maki on top of the cliff. "Thank you for calling me, Maki."

"Dr. Kujo, did you come alone?"

"Yes, I didn't tell anyone."

With a quiet determination, Maki confronted Kujo. "The antidote should be done by tomorrow."

"Really?"

"Professor Takahashi is going to tell the police everything. About how you were planning a terrorist attack, about how you killed my father. But—" Maki took a step forward. "Maybe you were planning to die from the start, Dr. Kujo."

Kujo nodded quietly, stone-faced.

"What I have to do now is get you to live so you can redeem yourself, so you can atone for your sins." It was what Maki had been contemplating ever since she had lost her father.

"Maki..." Kujo's eyes grew wider.

"My father always told me to never lose sight of what you have to do no matter what. And what I want is for you to take over my father's mission. So please, let's start over. If you can't—" Maki gripped the knife in her right hand. "I'll kill you, and then I'll kill myself."

Kujo looked around her and sighed. "That's why you asked to meet here. The virus won't spread, and we'll be the only ones to die."

Maki nodded. Her father had taught her the risks of working with deadly viruses, and that as his daughter she might one day have to sacrifice herself for others.

"Maki, you still believe in me? And forgive me after everything that's happened?"

Maki recalled the image of how her father had died. The woman her father trusted with his life, but who drove him to his death, now stood before her. For an instant, a burning hatred nearly erupted from her soul, but Maki extinguished it. "Maybe I can't forgive you yet. But I do believe in you."

Kujo looked away to gaze at the sea. Endless houses and streets spread out on the other side of the bay. It was a warm and peaceful scene. Maki stood next to Kujo, like she used to, and stared across the bay.

"Dr. Kujo, that place over there is filled with happiness. Of course, there are some bad people there, but still everyone is trying to live life to the fullest. Can you really destroy all that?"

Finally Kujo said, "All right, Maki. I'll bring everything out in the open. About killing your father. About what we have been trying to do."

"Dr. Kujo...thank you."

The two took a step closer and held each other's hand. Their hands became connected by a tiny hope that transcended despair, hate, and anguish.

"Maki, if we stay here—"

Kujo was interrupted by a car and a motorcycle speeding down the sandy path. They came to a halt blocking Kujo and Maki's escape. Matoba emerged from the back seat of the car, his face panic-stricken. "Dr. Kujo, it isn't safe to act alone," he said, "What would you have done if you had allowed the girl to escape? She is a valuable pawn. With her, we can counter L's Death Note."

"Mr. Matoba, I—" Kujo shielded Maki behind her back. When Kujo looked down at Maki's face, however, she knitted her brows and smiled as if she had cast off her emotions and put on another mask entirely. Then she thrust Maki out in front of Matoba. Kujo also held what resembled an ampule in her hand. "Mr. Matoba, we don't have just the girl. She brought the antidote with her. This should be more than enough to inoculate the whole of Blue Ship."

"Dr. Kujo—" Maki's cry was stifled by Matoba, who covered her mouth with a hand.

"Looks like Konishi's reverse eavesdropping plan paid off," Yoshizawa said.

"Call me Ohnishi," Konishi said.

As Maki was forced into the car, a shadowy figure came into her field of vision.

"Ryuzaki!"

The members all turned at once. L was pedaling furiously on a bicycle toward the cliff.

"Well now. The hero always arrives late to the dance. Only this time he's a little *too* late. We'll be taking the girl and the antidote now." With a nod toward Hatsune, Matoba climbed into the car. It peeled out in a cloud of dust and sand.

Hatsune drew the stiletto knife and licked the edge of the blade. L skidded to a halt on the bicycle, panting and carrying nothing but an umbrella.

"You think that's any good against me?" Like a wasp, the blade took a quick and graceful path toward its target and twined around L's sleeve. Blood spurted from L's right arm. His face twisted in pain. Ripping off the sleeve, L raised the umbrella as if it were an epee.

"Now I can move my arm better."

"Sore loser!" Hatsune lunged with the knife. L kept her at bay using the long reach of the umbrella. "Give! It! Up!" The blade sliced through the air three times. Hatsune angrily kicked the sand at her feet. L quickly stooped over and opened the one-touch umbrella in Hatsune's face.

"Not good enough!" The knife slashed through the nylon fabric of the umbrella. Then she was taken aback by what she saw through the tear. L's face was planted in the sand, like a frog that had lost its balance. He vaulted head over heels in a handspring and slammed both feet against Hatsune's shoulders. The stiletto sailed out of Hatsune's hand.

"Nice try, but there's no catching the car now." Hatsune rushed to her motorcycle, threw a leg over it, and waved goodbye. She kicked up a cloud of sand behind her as she sped off down the road.

L ran after the car that carried Maki. Straightening his curved back. Pushing his body beyond what it could handle. He knew from the start that there would be no catching up to them. That his own body was no match for a car. And still L ran. Like a man who had battled everything that was ludicrous in this world. Just like those who confronted a great evil in the name of justice. The car receded into the distance. L fell forward on his hands and knees gasping for breath.

"Light—this feeling of failing to protect those to whom you promised safety. Is this the reality you spoke of?"

The car's taillights gradually faded from view. The blood from the wound trickled down L's arm to the broken watch he wore in remembrance of Light and dripped onto the asphalt. Suddenly, he pounded his fist against the hard ground. Over and over. He did not stop even when his knuckles were pink with blood.

"Light…it hurts. My heart—"

It was a hurt that L. Lawleit had suppressed, that he had to suppress in order to continue his existence as the peerless Detective L. How had the world's top detective been described with regard to facets of his personality other than his ability as a detective? He had been called a kinky detective who relished bizarre murders, a human computer capable only of measuring mass murders in terms of cold numbers, a reclusive sociopath. What L thought of such estimations of his personality only L could know. But no one could truly understand L. How L did not and could not forget the faces of thousands of victims. Who could comprehend the man who had lived his life, and had to live confronting all of the lives ended prematurely, the tears of the grief-stricken survivors, the devaluing of life as a daily reality. How was it possible to measure the pain of such a man?

Was it a strain so heavy that L's back curved under all its weight? Was it an agony so terrible to leave the indelible dark circles around his eyes? Was it a feeling so bitter that every bite he took needed to be coated in sugar? The chronically rounded shoulders, the inevitable dark circles, the eccentric tastes—L suppressed the pain of being a champion of justice, but the evidence of the pain was molded into his very body.

L tore out his hair and howled at the sky, unleashing the agony inside his soul.

L 02-2 Deception

When L returned to the pier, Suruga was waiting for him inside the red takoyaki truck.

"What happened to Maki?" Suruga asked. But he took one look at L's arm and realized what had happened. "She wasn't—"

"Regrettably yes." Seeing L quietly enduring the pain, Suruga couldn't bear to press him further. After a minute, L finally turned his attention to the familiar figure standing there, unable to join in the conversation. "And what might you be doing here?" L asked.

"That hurts, especially since you're the one who called me here." Matsuda of the Metropolitan Police stuck out his lips sullenly.

"Me? Are you saying that I called you here?"

"Huh? I mean, the 'L' appeared on my computer and instructed me to deliver the transmitted data to his location in Osaka so…" Matsuda held out a printout of a report.

"The other L?" Suruga asked, rubbing the stubble on his face. Matsuda looked alternately at L and Suruga, confused. But L did not offer an answer as he began to riffle through the pages of the report. Then he looked up and smiled. "It seems the puzzle has been solved."

Looking down at his watch, Suruga reported, "Ryuzaki, we received a message from someone with Blue Ship named Yoshizawa while you were gone. He wants both of us to go to the thirtieth floor of the Umeda New Sky Building at six o'clock tonight."

"The thirtieth floor…at six?"

"Yeah, plus he gave us two conditions: bring the Death Note and keep the FBI out of it. Now that they have Maki as a hostage, suddenly they're playing hardball."

"May I have a moment to think about this?" L squatted down and began to bite his nails. He mumbled repeatedly, "Thirtieth floor… six o'clock…Death Note…" Finally he stood up and declared, "We should go. Will you assist us, Mr. Matsuda?"

"What, me too?" Matsuda was wary of being embroiled in circumstances he knew little about.

"Yes. There is a job only you can do for us."

"Oh. Got it!" The ever-naïve Matsuda seemed enthused by the fact that his skills were needed.

"Mr. Suruga, I'd like you to grab one of the FBI agents watching over us. They will have a part in this as well."

"But Blue Ship warned us not to get the FBI involved."

"They just can't show themselves, that's all. You're welcome to scare them a little if you'd like."

"All right."

†

The preparations were complete. As L, Suruga, and Matsuda were getting ready to climb into the takoyaki truck, Takahashi handed L a small case.

"It's a sample of the antidote. There's only enough there for one person. It hasn't been tested, so I don't know if it's effective."

"Thank you, Professor Takahashi. Please continue to work on the antidote. We will soon require large quantities of it. I will be sure to send someone for it when the time comes."

"All right. But send someone for it...what are you—" L answered with a shake of his head.

"Ryuzaki, Suruga, get our Maki back!" Takahashi shouted as the truck sped off. L thrust his arm out the window and gave a thumbs-up.

"The thirtieth of floor of the Umeda New Sky Building. What do you think is waiting for us there, Ryuzaki?"

"That they designated a high rise in the middle of Osaka as the meeting place must mean Blue Ship is executing their plan to wipe out Japan. In all likelihood, they have replicated the virus in an aerosolized form and intend to spray it from the thirtieth floor of the building. The time of six p.m. is so the virus weapon can cause the greatest damage without being hampered by the sunlight. The building is located between Osaka and Umeda Stations, which ensures heavy foot traffic. By the time of the onset of the virus two weeks from now, the people who have become carriers will have dispersed all across the country. Japan will literally be wiped out."

"But is aerial dispersion really all that effective? Sure, the virus is likely to enter the lungs of passersby outside. But every air-conditioned building has its windows closed during the summer. Maybe the virus won't spread as much as we think," Suruga said.

L shook his head. "Mr. Suruga, there are hundreds of millions of virus cells in a single drop of blood. Even in a sealed building, a relative handful of virus cells entering the air-conditioning system would be enough to infect everyone in the building." L took out a crumpled picture of Watari from his jeans pocket. "Watari. Perhaps my death won't be as 'quiet' as I had hoped."

Observing L from the backseat, Matsuda asked, "But isn't your fate already decided by what was written in the Death Note?"

"No, it only means that what was written in the Death Note cannot be overturned by another entry. If someone were to shoot me right now, I would probably die."

"Oh—"

"It's all right. With your assistance, I will be able to die a peaceful death as written." L turned around and directed a sad smile at Matsuda, who was worried for him. "At any rate, Matoba said something odd back at the cliff. That he had the antidote in his possession. It seems Dr. Kujo has tricked the Blue Ship members into believing that she obtained the antidote from Maki."

"What's going on? Is Kujo betraying the group? For what purpose?" Behind the wheel, Suruga frowned as he stroked his chin.

"I don't know. But she appears to have a different agenda than that of Matoba." L pulled out the report that Matsuda had brought him. "Mr. Suruga, do you recall the incident about nine months ago—270 days ago, to be exact, with Robert Fairman, the FBI infiltrator?"

"Fairman? Yeah, that was some ordeal. But how do you know about that?"

"I was at the scene."

"At the scene? Hey, come to think of it, that Bear's Crepe truck—"

"The confidential files that Fairman attempted to steal pertained to a mysterious explosion at an infectious disease lab in 1980. The files contained evidence to prove that the research lab was destroyed to conceal its development of virus weapons." L continued, "It would have caused quite a scandal for the United States, which has openly declared that it would not develop virus weapons."

"What does that have to do with what's going on now?"

"Dr. Kujo's parents were working at the infectious disease lab. Although they weren't involved with the research of virus weapons, somehow they became entangled in the incident."

"Which means Kujo has a vendetta against the United States, is that it?"

"The identity of whoever was pulling Fairman's strings and issued fake orders from the secretary of state has yet to be found. But one fact has been revealed."

"What is it?"

"We received word that Fairman left the U.S. several days ago and entered Japan under the alias Gilbert Vine. Perhaps there is a connection."

"Tell me, Ryuzaki, who is the report from?"

L looked down at the report and smiled as if he were remembering its author. "From someone who likes to solve puzzles."

†

Osaka Station and the north side of the shopping district were visible from the thirtieth-floor window of the Umeda New Sky Building. Yoshizawa and Hatsune greeted L and Suruga inside the vacant office at gunpoint, oozing with superiority.

"So let's have the Death Note. If you hesitate here, I'll have the girl killed," Yoshizawa said.

"I understand. I'll give you the notebook." L obediently held out a bag of potato chips. Suruga rolled his eyes over L's unconventional storage methods, and apparently Yoshizawa felt similarly as he took the bag suspiciously and pulled out the notebook.

"Now Detective, there are supposed to be two Death Notes according to you. Where is the other one?"

"That was a bluff. I burned the other Death Note."

Yoshizawa and even Suruga directed a doubtful eye at L's aloof face. "I don't trust you. In the first place, if you destroy the Death Note by burning, everyone who's ever touched it will die."

"The thirteen-day rule and the rule that anyone who touches the notebook will die if it were burned are dummy rules created by Kira to throw off the investigation. I can burn that one too if you'd like."

Yoshizawa pulled the Death Note away from L, who looked like he might pull out a lighter any moment. "No, you've burned us enough times already. Never mind that, we'll prove whether this notebook is genuine or not right now."

"Right now? You're not thinking of—"

"Good guess, FBI," said Hatsune, opening the notebook. "That's right, you two are going to write your own names in the Death Note."

Suruga looked to L for help. Perhaps sensing Suruga's expectation of a brilliant maneuver, L began rather proudly, "Think about it from their perspective, Mr. Suruga. If they allow us to live, we might try to stop their plan, and they need to confirm whether the Death Note is genuine or not anyhow. Forcing us to write our own names is the most practical way to accomplish both."

"Oh, right…guess so." Suruga's shoulders sank. Yoshizawa and Hatsune exchanged a glance, suspicious that the notebook might be fake judging from how cheerful L seemed to be.

"Well then, Detective, you first." Yoshizawa handed the notebook and pen to L.

After looking up in thought, L faced Yoshizawa and said, "If you write the cause of death, you will die as written; otherwise, you will die by heart attack. Heart attack is such a painful way to die. May I write another cause of death?"

Before Yoshizawa could answer otherwise, L had written his name and cause of death, holding the pen unsteadily by its end.

"H-hey, Ryuzaki. Did you really write in the notebook? What, death by falling?" After peering over L's shoulder at the Death Note, Suruga shook L by the shoulder.

"Mr. Suruga, I am the world's top detective. If there is no hope of achieving victory, I must accept defeat. Goodbye, Mr. Suru—gah!" Forty seconds had elapsed mid-sentence. L darted to the window and jumped like it was a walk in the park.

"Did he really jump?" Yoshizawa looked down from the veranda and saw L sprawled on the asphalt of the parking lot below. He looked like a frog that had been flattened by a car. The body did not move an inch. "He's dead…The notebook is real."

"Well, that was manly of him. Now it's your turn, FBI." Hatsune smiled and held out the Death Note in Suruga's direction. After appearing to accept his fate, Suruga began to write down his name.

Yoshizawa, who'd been looking over Suruga's shoulder, pointed the gun at Suruga. "Now, FBI. Kujo already found out that your real name is Hideaki Sugita. Stop stalling and write it down already.

Otherwise, I'll just have to shoot you dead myself."

"I have a request to make. Will you give me a little time?"

"Huh? What are you talking about?"

"The Death Note allows you to designate the exact cause and time of death. I could die in my sleep and have a little more time to think back on my life first."

Yoshizawa shook his head wearily. "Nice try. Unfortunately, we have to be on our way to the airport to leave the country. Not to mention, the way L died just now, the police will soon be here. We can't rest easy until we watch you die."

"That's right. You're liable to call the police or disable the virus dispersion device before you die."

Suruga said, "Think about it. L just jumped to his death in what looks like a suicide. When the police get here, they're bound to investigate the upper floors from where he might have jumped. It would look suspicious if they found my body in this room at the same time. And if you're not careful, they might find your dispersion device and disable it." Yoshizawa and Hatsune exchanged leery glances. Suruga appeared to have a point. Suruga opened the notebook to the rules page. "Look, it says here that you can manipulate the circumstances leading up to the death. I can write that I won't try to contact anyone once you leave and that I won't open the door when the police get here. And I'll write that I won't touch your device. Listen to a dying man's wish. I'm not prepared to die like L did. I'm begging you!" Suruga dropped down and threw himself at Yoshizawa's feet.

Yoshizawa eyed his watch. "All right. You have two hours. I don't want the trouble of the police investigating this room. But write this down in the notebook: Hideaki Sugita will die quietly on July 28th, 20:30 without contacting anyone, leaving this room, or tampering with the virus dispersion device."

"A-all right." Suruga tried to still his trembling hand as he wrote in the notebook. Then he looked around in a daze, as if he could not recognize the imminence of his irreversible fate.

Hatsune flopped down in front of him and peered into his face. "Goodbye, FBI. It was fun while it lasted."

"Your underwear's showing again."

"My parting gift to you," she said, with a wink and smile.

"Rest in peace, FBI. The virus dispersion device is set to activate twenty minutes after your death. Then you and L will be the ones blamed for perpetrating a terrorist attack. Lucky for you to go out with a bang."

Yoshizawa and Hatsune left the room, leaving Suruga sitting slumped on the floor. Alone now, he went to the window and looked down at the city, painted orange by the setting sun. The siren of an ambulance that likely carried L faded into the distance and was drowned out by the bustle of the city.

†

"Dang, I don't ever want to get stuck with this role again. Stupid Ryuzaki!" Matsuda, disguised in a white long-sleeve shirt and jeans, tore off the wig and threw it down as soon as he entered the room.

"You were a great help. And you played an excellent corpse." Having just returned from the twenty-ninth floor, L cocked his head at Matsuda, who was dressed just like him. Even Suruga could not keep from laughing out loud.

"I bet they couldn't imagine that we'd try to give them a fake Death Note now," Suruga said.

"Mr. Suruga, please give the FBI my thanks. From the agents who caught my fall with a mattress on the 29th floor, to the men who put Mr. Matsuda in the ambulance, I'm grateful. And please inform them that they no longer need to watch us on the president's orders. And that I won't be writing the president's name in the Death Note no matter what happens in the next two days."

"Sure, I'll go tell them."

After Suruga left the room, Matsuda let out an exaggerated sigh. "It was a nice trap, Ryuzaki, but was it necessary to go through such an elaborate ruse?"

"It was the only way to get close to the virus dispersion device without bringing harm to Maki. My death was the only way to get them to believe the Death Note was real and to get them to leave without actually witnessing Suruga die."

L walked out onto the veranda to examine the virus dispersion device. "It appears to be a rudimentary contraption made from a virus replication tank, pump, motor, and an electric fan. The timer set on the motor allows the terrorists ample time to make their getaway."

"Such a simple-looking device." Matsuda reached out a hand, which L swatted away with all his might. "Ow!"

"You mustn't be so careless with it. Contained in this device is enough of the virus to kill the entire population of Japan."

"With this thing?" Matsuda said, amazed. It was the same tone of voice he'd had when in the same room with the Death Note for the first time.

"That's right. With this thing." L was suddenly grave. "There is nothing acceptable about being able to take human life so easily." L ripped out the cord from the motor. "We'll close off access to this room and call in the Osaka Police's NBC Terrorism Task Force. We must go to the airport. We might be able to use your sharpshooting skills, Mr. Matsuda."

"Leave it to me. Let's go!"

†

"But how does Kujo plan to get Maki on a plane? Everyone in the country knows she's been infected with the virus, and the airport is

160

bound to be on high alert as well. Not to mention that Matoba and the others are internationally wanted terrorists," Suruga said as he started the takoyaki truck.

"I'm accessing the internal network at Kansai International Airport." L, in the passenger seat, typed away on the computer, hacked into the airport system, and began to take in the information that came up onscreen. "Here it is. There is a request for an emergency transport of a patient on UA Flight 718 departing for Los Angeles at 20:50."

"Emergency transport?"

"Dr. Kujo plans to take Maki to the States by disguising her as a patient in need of an emergency operation. Matoba and the others will likely board the same flight posing as doctors and nurses. Smuggling weapons and bombs inside the medical equipment should be easy enough. They also have the added advantage of being able to use the plane as a bioweapon were Maki or Dr. Kujo to exhibit symptoms during the flight."

"If the plane were to explode over American airspace, the virus would rain down from the sky. In which case Kujo and Matoba as well as the Blue Ship members will all go up in flames."

"Dr. Kujo may well be prepared for that eventuality. While the Blue Ship members intend to escape the threat of the virus, Dr. Kujo may be planning to annihilate the United States by using the members themselves as viral weapons."

"A suicide attack to exact vengeance on the United States for killing her parents."

"But Ryuzaki, wasn't this Kujo woman infiltrating Nikaido's lab?" Matsuda asked from the back seat. "She should have had plenty of opportunity to steal the virus without Blue Ship's help. Why would she have to smuggle the virus into the U.S. in such a roundabout way?"

"Perhaps the U.S. is not Kujo's target of revenge."

"Huh? What do you mean by that?"

"We should have an answer to the entire puzzle at the airport."

"A 20:50 departure. It'll take us a while to get there from here," Suruga said, rubbing the stubble on his chin.

"We have no other choice. Let's go, Mr. Suruga, Mr. Matsuda!"

Suruga, who was used to driving the truck by now, wove though the shopping district according to the female voice of the GPS.

—Go straight at right-turn lane ahead, turn left simultaneously with red light, drive down sidewalk at second utility pole, turn 90 feet ahead, drive over 40mph against traffic down one-way street.—

"Damn, if she isn't getting demanding!" Suruga cursed, managing to maneuver the truck as instructed nevertheless.

"Don't rock the truck, you're spilling the sauce." L popped another takoyaki drowned in chocolate sauce into his mouth. Suruga scowled, but L had on a stern look that Suruga had never seen before. In his own way, snacking was L's method of preparing for action.

†

After committing about 120 points worth of traffic violations, Suruga spied the red flashing lights of a police car in the rearview mirror. "Ryuzaki, they're coming!"

"They would be pretty incompetent if they didn't pursue a reckless takoyaki truck."

"Don't sound so calm!"

"We'll try to throw them off. Go into that shopping arcade over there."

"Go into—that's..." It was the arcade inside Shinsaibashi, the busiest street in Osaka. With just a glance at the red lights closing in on the truck in the rearview mirror, Suruga pointed the truck at the arcade and honked the horn.

The shopping arcade was bustling with activity on a summer

night. While the relatively small truck managed to thread its way through the throngs of people, the police car with its sirens blaring closed the gap as the people moved aside.

"They're gaining on us, Ryuzaki. What should we do?"

L took out a bag that he had brought with him. "These items might come in handy. Slow down, Mr. Suruga."

"Slow down? If I do that—"

"It's all right." With a few taps on the computer, L connected to the truck's controls, launched an audio file, and turned on the external sound system. Suddenly "The Wind of Mount Rokko," the Hanshin Tigers' team anthem, blasted out of the speakers at full volume. The Osakans, for whom rooting for the Tigers was a part of their genetic makeup, began to look curiously at the careening truck.

Grabbing the microphone, L began to speak in a faux Osaka dialect. "Gather around folks! A special gift for all of you Tigers fans out there. Collectible items autographed by the Tigers players, only while supplies last!" L snatched the autographed bats, gloves, and uniforms out of the bag and tossed them into the crowd.

In an instant, rabid fans thronged around the truck, the area erupting into a scene like the one at Dotonbori when the Tigers won a championship. The police siren was drowned out amid the Tigers' anthem and the clamor of the crowd, and the police car could no longer move in any direction.

"Where did you get that stuff, Ryuzaki?" Suruga asked.

"I bought it at an Internet auction. I planned to give it to Maki as a gift but…" L looked at the autographed ball Maki had wanted and tossed it into the crowd. "We should go, Mr. Suruga."

"R-right." The takoyaki truck sped off again, stranding the police car behind them.

"Smooth sailing, Ryuzaki!"

"Mr. Suruga, this may not be the appropriate time, but may I make a confession?"

"What is it all of a sudden?"

"I regret to tell you that no real Death Note exists. I burned both of them after Kira's death."

Suruga gave L a long confused look. The truck nearly veered off the sidewalk, and he hastily put his eyes back on the road. "There's no real Death Note? Then why did you hide it like it was so valuable? And why did I go through all the trouble of recovering it?"

"I don't ever recall saying that the Death Note in my possession was real," said L innocently. Indeed he had not once said that he had the genuine Death Note; neither had he once said that he didn't. Suruga's heart sank. His infiltration of the Kira Investigation Headquarters, the performance with Kujo back at the Yellow Box warehouse, and the dangerous mission to recover the Death Note from Blue Ship had all been for naught.

"Hold on. You wrote down the name of a criminal in the Death Note in order to threaten the president and he died. What kind of trick was that?"

"After Misa Amane, who was the second Kira, was released from confinement, she resumed the killings as Kira—with the real Death Note on the first day, but with a fake book starting the second day after Watari had made the switch."

"Yeah, that much I read about in your report to the FBI. Which was why the only deaths following Amane's release happened on that first day."

"Among those whose names were written on that first day was one criminal who had not yet died. I omitted this detail from the report."

"Written in the Death Note, but not dead—how is that possible?" Suruga did not bother to hide his irritation.

"It was simply a case of Misa Amane writing in the wrong date. The date she had mistakenly written was July 23."

"The exact date and time you told the president."

"What was already written in the Death Note could not be altered. I knew that the U.S. government and the FBI were wary of my connection with the Death Note. I withheld this information about the mistaken date from my report so I might use it in an emergency. Also, that threat to force the president to launch nuclear weapons isn't possible either. The Death Note cannot be used to kill in a way that involves killing others. I neglected to include that detail in the report as well…"

Though the trick was now clear, Suruga was not yet entirely satisfied. "Then why didn't you say as much to the president? That both Death Notes had been destroyed and that the person threatening the president was a fake L. It was hardly necessary to go along with the impostor's methods. We were nearly killed because of it."

L did not offer an answer as he trained his sights on the road ahead. To Suruga, L seemed to be studying a chessboard and looking hundreds of moves ahead.

𝕃02-3 Hope

The wave-shaped terminal of Kansai International Airport was lit up against the night sky. Blue guide lights along the runway spread out like a sea of fireflies as airplanes jetted off one after the next.

Having pulled away from the gate on time, UA Flight 718 for Los Angeles crept slowly toward the runway. Inside the business class cabin, Maki, made to look like a patient in need of an emergency surgery, slept on a specially installed bed. The bed was blocked off from the rest of the cabin by a curtain. Kujo, dressed in a long white physician's coat and sitting next to Maki, kept a close watch on the girl from the other side of the curtain. Relaxing in the seat next to Kujo was Matoba, who also wore a doctor's coat with a satisfied air.

"It was touch-and-go for a moment, but everything appears to be going as planned," Matoba said. "We brought the girl to guard against L, but that might have been an unnecessary precaution." Matoba looked down on Maki as if she were a lab animal, then glanced at his watch. "The virus dispersion device should be activated by now. By the onset of the symptoms in two weeks' time, the virus will have spread across the country. Professor Nikaido's name will go down in history as the devil who wrought the annihilation of Japan," Matoba said joyously. He smiled as if the plan's success were all but assured.

"Yes," replied Kujo, smiling quietly.

Matoba detected something unnatural in her expression. "Is something the matter, Dr. Kujo? You don't seem quite yourself."

Kujo shook her head. "When I think about how our plan is very nearly a reality, I suppose I'm a little emotional. And I seem to be coming down with a cold. I'm a little feverish." Kujo's eyes looked watery.

"Oh, is that so? Fortunately, we have some time until we arrive in America. I hope you'll get some rest on the plane." Kujo nodded and checked on Maki on the other side of the curtain. There was a ping overhead, which was followed by an announcement.

"Ladies and gentleman, this is your captain speaking. The control tower has instructed us to hold our position. It appears a vehicle has wandered onto the runway."

Kujo looked out the window as she asked, "May I ask you a question, Mr. Matoba?"

As suspicious as he was of her unusual behavior, he answered, "Of course."

"Do you recall the mysterious explosion of an infectious disease lab on East Serras Island in 1980, twenty-six years ago?"

Although it was old history, Matoba's reply was immediate. "Of course I remember. That job was something of a debut for me in this business. An efficient job, as I recall. After all, the cover-up itself was orchestrated by the American government."

Kujo continued without a hint of emotion. "Then I suppose there were three truths covered up in that incident. One, virus weapons were being developed at the research facility, and two, in order to conceal that, the U.S. government blew up the facility along with its researchers. Three, the biohazard, which was a direct cause of the explosion, was a terrorist act linked with the presidential elections—"

"You've done your research," Matoba said, impressed. No doubt Kujo had looked into Matoba's history prior to teaming up with him. There was little reason for Matoba to feel bad about having been investigated. After all, this was a world where yesterday's enemy could become today's ally. If Kujo were not as cautious as Matoba, she would hardly qualify to partner with him.

"Mr. Matoba, would you mind explaining how you infiltrated the facility. For future reference?"

Matoba crossed the other leg and thought back to the time twenty-six years ago. "There was an Asian couple among the researchers working there. We were close in age, so we became fast friends. We threw parties and went camping together with our families, and they shared some valuable information. The security in the lab, vulnerabilities of the security staff, the firearms the guards were equipped with—"

"Do you recall an eight-year-old girl in that family?"

"Why yes. An adorable little girl. I felt sorry for her." Kujo's shoulders twitched at his almost nostalgic tone. It was then that Matoba realized that Kujo was speaking of details that she could not have researched. The eight-year-old girl, all those years ago...He attempted to superimpose the girl's innocent smiling face over that of the woman before him. There was no resemblance. Yet Matoba sensed something. "You're not...?"

Yoshizawa and Hatsune forced their way past a flight attendant and rushed to where Kujo and Matoba sat. "Mr. Matoba! L is in the vehicle on the runway!"

"What? You said L was dead."

"Yes, we were certain of it!" Hatsune pulled back the curtain to look out the window, and her heart stopped. "She has the symptoms!"

Maki moaned in pain as a bloody tear trickled down her face.

"What's happening, Dr. Kujo? You were supposed to have given her the antidote," Matoba lashed out.

Kujo looked at Maki and dropped her head. "I was hoping to keep up the charade until we were over the United States." Suddenly she stood up and looked across the cabin of the plane. "Fairman, Konishi, switch to Plan B! Let's move!"

Konishi, who had come up to check in, pushed Yoshizawa and Hatsune aside and rushed to Maki's bedside. He pulled out the guns stowed away in the medical equipment next to the bed. The man who had been idly leafing through a magazine in the row ahead jumped to his feet and took the gun from Konishi.

"We are taking control of the plane!" the man announced in English, then in Japanese. His voice sounded odd. He leveled the gun at the passengers. Keeping a watchful eye on the cabin, he asked Kujo, "What happened? We were supposed to make our move after we took off."

"Fairman, L is here. Take control of the cockpit and get us out of here!"

"Right!" Fairman tore off the beard, removed the stuffing out of his cheeks, and winked at Matoba. "It's been a while, Matoba.

Although, I guess I'm supposed to be dead. Think of me as a ghost with a grudge. This time you may not get off with just a scar."

Fairman headed for the cockpit as Konishi took over watching the hostages. Matoba's hand traced the burn scar on his cheek. "I thought he died in Brunei…"

"Yes, instead of you. It seems all the enemies you made in the past have finally caught up with you." Kujo laughed and fixed her eyes on Matoba. "Can you believe that little girl from twenty-six years ago has been waiting for the chance to exact revenge on the American government and the ringleader of that cover-up?"

Matoba could only stand there in shock. Just as Kujo had investigated Matoba's past, Matoba had also checked Kujo's history. "But Dr. Kujo, we had your—"

"I appreciate your being so easily duped by my fictionalized past." She bowed in mock deference. Finally Matoba realized that the woman before him had an agenda utterly her own. Kujo continued, "Oh yes. I forgot to tell you. That drug I injected all of you with wasn't the antidote. It was the virus. Which makes all of the members onboard carriers of the virus."

Matoba stared dumbly. His expression, eyes wide, jaw nearly to his chest, was a far cry from his usual affected self. "What about how you obtained the antidote from the girl?"

"I never obtained the antidote."

"So not only is the girl infected, we are all ticking bombs of the virus?" "Kujo!" Matoba advanced in Kujo's direction.

"Did you really think that I believed in your fairy tale about a world for a chosen few?"

"Fairy tale?" Having lost all semblance of composure, Matoba simply blubbered and twitched.

Kujo confronted Matoba with a cynical smile. "This was my mission all along. To lead you to the depths of despair just before your plan was on the brink of success. And I will change the world, just as you desired. By making you the virus bomb."

"Damn you!" Matoba lunged at Kujo. But he relaxed his grip on her upon seeing her face. He began to inch backward.

A single bloody tear trickled from Kujo's bloodshot eyes. It was the first stage of the onset of the virus.

"It looks like I'm beginning to show symptoms." As Kujo wept bloody tears, a smile came across her face.

"N-no! Get away! Help me! I don't want to die!" Matoba said. "I don't want to die, I don't..." he said again and again. He collapsed on the floor and continued to retreat on his backside until he bumped into Hatsune's legs.

"What an ass." For all Hatsune had respected, even worshipped, the man, her change in attitude was all the more drastic after witnessing Matoba's humiliating display. Hatsune looked at Kujo, who pointed a gun at her, and shrugged. "Do it, if you want. I won't fight you. I knew all along that you were badder than the rest of us." She turned her back on Kujo and returned to her seat, humming a song.

"What the hell is going on, Konishi? We're all going to die," Yoshizawa said.

"Oh, did you have it in your mind that you'd survive, Yoshizawa? Only the elite who are necessary to the new world survive," Konishi jeered.

"What are you so high and mighty for? Since when did you become Kujo's lackey, you nerdy bastard!" Yoshizawa didn't care about Konishi's gun. All he saw was the meek computer nerd.

Though Konishi continued to stare at Yoshizawa with unfocussed eyes, his laugh grew into a dissonant screech. "You always mocked me, called me a geek! And rode me and rode me!" Konishi's eyes took on a dangerous glint. The gun in his trembling hand was aimed at Yoshizawa's chest.

"W-wait! I-I'm sorry!" Yoshizawa realized for the first time that he had pressed a button he dared not in a weak-kneed man, but it was already too late.

"You deserve to die!"

Konishi squeezed the trigger once, twice, three times in all. And Yoshizawa crumpled to the floor in his own pool of blood.

Meanwhile Fairman ripped the microphone away from the flight attendant's hand and announced, "Ladies and gentlemen, this is your hijacker speaking. I'm afraid we're going to be spending the next several hours together. First, you should know that we are not only armed with guns but with enough plastic explosives to blow up this plane. The one with the finger on the switch is sitting somewhere in this cabin. If anyone attempts to resist, that person will hit the switch without a moment's hesitation. We are also in possession of another weapon. You might have heard the news of a deadly virus. A patient who already has symptoms of that virus is onboard this plane, and you are all already infected with it. If you resist us and somehow manage to escape, know that the antidote does not exist in Japan. However, if you come quietly to the U.S. with us, we promise you will receive proper treatment along with the antidote. I urge you to keep this in mind and act accordingly."

The plastic explosives and the claim that the antidote would be available in the U.S. were bluffs, but it was enough to quiet the hostages.

Fairman then ordered the flight attendant to patch him through to the cockpit. "Captain, as you may have heard, the passengers aboard this plane are as good as dead if we don't fly to the U.S. So do as I say, and quietly."

Once the door was unlocked, Fairman entered the cockpit, tied up the pilot and copilot, and took over the pilot's seat. "All of the preparations have been made for this day. Get a load of what we've got planned for the U.S." Fairman cursed. "Chewing people up just as fast as they can spit them out. We've got a very special present for that no-good country."

Slowly the airplane slid forward toward the runway.

As the passengers grappled with the reality of the hijacking and virus, the cabin was enveloped in an eerie silence. Fairman's announcement was proving effective; no one appeared to make any sign of resistance.

"I'm sorry, Maki, for involving you in all of this." Kujo sat back down at Maki's bedside and gently stroked her head. "But by the time you're an adult, this earth will be a world devoid of dreams and hope, ruled only by despair. You're better off going to heaven now to be with your parents."

Maki tried to gather her thoughts, muddled by a high fever. "I won't give up on my life, and I won't give up on the future of this earth. I have to live...for my mother and father." A voice that refused to abandon hope. It was only a source of agony for Kujo now. "Besides, Ryuzaki promised to save me. I believe in him. You shouldn't give up hope either, Dr. Kujo...it's always possible to start over."

Kujo tried to still her wavering heart and answered, "It's too late. We have already hijacked this plane. We're about to take off and are headed for America; we're both infected. We will wipe out the U.S. and then annihilate the world. This world has no need for humanity anymore."

After Hatsune left Kujo, she started listlessly thumbing through a magazine. She did not even bat an eye when Yoshizawa's death was made known to her by gunshots just after she had returned to her seat. Death was a mere trifle to Hatsune, who had killed her first victim at fifteen. People always stood on the precipice between life and death, and death was nothing more than a result of a tiny change of balance. Hatsune was simply incapable of being affected by the death of a stranger, a loved one, or even herself.

Then she realized that nothing she read from the magazine had sunk in.

He was stupid, but we did make a good team...

Hatsune got up and pulled out an umbrella from her carry-on luggage. She unraveled the tape wrapped around the tip of the umbrella to reveal that the handle had been shaved into a sharp plastic spike.

"Move it." Hatsune pushed a flight attendant out of the way and heaved open the emergency exit. The wind blasted inside the cabin and the passengers began to scream. The flight attendant tumbled to the floor, and inflight magazines, true to their name, fluttered around the interior of the cabin.

As she readied herself to jump onto the wing of the airplane, Konishi rushed at her with a gun in hand. "Hatsune, w-where do you think you're going?"

"I'm bored, so I'm getting off. See ya!" she shouted over the din.

Konishi raised his gun. "S-stop..."

"Hm, a little high. These heels have to go." Hatsune broke off the heels of her high-heeled shoes and prepared to jump.

"I'll shoot." Konishi pointed the gun at Hatsune's chest.

Hatsune eyed the gun as if a sidewalk survey-taker had inconveniently thrust a clipboard in her face. Suddenly she kicked the barrel of the gun upward. A shot went off toward the ceiling. Without even lowering her foot, Hatsune promptly kicked the gun a second time as Konishi stumbled, and knocked it out the door.

Konishi let out a terrified cry. Flopping on the floor, he began to retreat on his backside. "Hatsune...I'm sorry...pl—"

"Aw, shut up." Having lost all interest in Konishi, Hatsune took the fastest method of silencing him. The umbrella penetrated deep inside his throat and stilled Konishi from ever speaking again. "Don't hesitate if you're going to shoot, you nerdy bastard."

†

By the time Hatsune opened the emergency exit, Suruga had

pulled the takoyaki truck alongside the moving plane.

"Aim for the door, Mr. Matsuda!" L shouted from atop the roof of the truck.

"Okay!" Matsuda leaned his body out the passenger seat, aimed the harpoon gun, and pulled the trigger. The harpoon attached to a rope line pierced the open door of the plane.

"Well done, Mr. Matsuda. Your sharp shooting skills alone are reliable."

"Alone..."

L clambered up the rope, his feet leaving the roof of the truck, as the wind blew him about. The wounded right arm was weak and slipped off the rope. The rope swung in front of the jet engine, nearly sending L into the turbine.

"Go, Ryuzaki!" Matsuda's cheers were carried out of L's earshot by the wind.

"Hrgh!" Righting himself, L mustered all his strength to climb the rope. He grabbed the edge of the wing with one hand. Then a shoe came down on it hard.

"I should have killed you when I had the chance." Hatsune wobbled clumsily as the plane accelerated, lifting her heel from L's hand.

"Who do you think you are, Mary Poppins?" Though L mocked the woman standing over him with an umbrella, his eyes were trained on the sharp end of the handle.

"See? It's even sharp enough to stab someone." Hatsune smiled and took aim with the umbrella between her fingers, as it if were a pool cue.

"Then you won't be needing this back." L let go of the wing. He disappeared under the wing, swinging like the weight at the end of a pendulum. When he swung back up to reappear before Hatsune, he gripped her stiletto knife in his hand. He evaded Hatsune's umbrella thrust and plunged the knife clear through the arch of her foot.

174

Hatsune let out a scream loud enough to be heard over the whine of the engines. Then she lost her balance and fell.

"Tit for tat." L watched her tumble down the runway, climbed up onto the wing, and crept toward the inside of the plane. The plane slowly picked up speed as Suruga followed on the cable and then made his way to the wing. The wind blowing in from the emergency exit whipped throughout the cabin.

L stayed low and hunched over, nearly walking on all fours. He made his way to the medical cabin and smiled at Kujo. He held an ampule in his hand. "Let Maki go, Dr. Kujo. I have only one dose of the antidote. Stop involving her in your affairs."

Kujo grabbed Maki from her sickbed and held the girl in her arms as if she were a shield. "Why do you try to save people?" Kujo wasn't surprised or angry; if anything her face betrayed a sense of pity. "The world's top detective, L. How much better is the world because of you? How much closer is the world to becoming a fair and just place under the law? Just how may lives has the law saved?" Kujo's voice cracked from anger and from the swiftly sinking air pressure in the cabin.

L stood before her, unflinching. "People aren't perfect. And neither is the law; it was created by imperfect people. But the law is the essence of people's desire to protect those they love, those they value. If there is even one person who continues to have hope in justice, I will continue to believe in justice under the law and protect it. For as long as I am L."

To Kujo, it was nothing more than the chivalrous ravings of a mad knight tilting at windmills. "How is it that you continue to have hope in humanity? After all the human folly and ugliness you've witnessed. And to still be able to believe in people, what a fool you are!"

"Dr. Kujo, is your time at Wammy's House perhaps a cause of your despair toward mankind?"

"You knew?"

"One can always tell a Wammy's student, even if they do change their face and hide their past," L said.

"If you knew who I was, then you should also know the reason for my actions."

"I do not," L answered bluntly. "I know that an operation you carried out led to your leaving Wammy's. But that operation—"

"Don't!" Kujo screamed. She looked away from L, her face twisted with self-loathing. "The operation was a success. But I made an error in the endgame. The hostage we saved turned out to be a child of the terrorist plotter, and the child's suicide attack was what the terrorists had planned all along. There were many casualties. I failed Watari's trust…"

The memories of the days after she had fled Wammy's House at sixteen flashed before her eyes. The overconfidence, the oversized ideals, her repeated failures…Amidst the futility of trying to change the world alone, Kujo's soul had grown darker than the world around it.

"Why do you think that?" L asked curiously. L, the overprotected, carefree detective, had taken up her position of mobilizing the law enforcement agencies of the world after Kujo abandoned Wammy's.

Kujo glared at him for mocking her. But L was smiling gently. The smile reminded her of someone. Someone she had not seen in years.

"Dr. Kujo, are you aware that you had been assigned a letter by Wammy's?"

Kujo's eyes grew larger. "Why? Assigning a letter to someone who abandoned Wammy's? That's impossible."

The designation of a letter in Wammy's alphabet held a special significance for those who graduated Wammy's House. It signified that they were charged with changing the world. There were only twenty-six letters to exist every generation, and these young people were part of an illustrious list of past letters who had time and again been instrumental in saving the world from catastrophe. Above all,

the designation signified Watari's trust.

"You are Wammy's K. Your letter was taken from Watari's last message to you before you left."

"Watari's message…" Kujo echoed in a raspy voice. A door, which had long been closed, seemed to open again.

L smiled, mischievously at first and then respectfully at the woman and letter who came before him. "KEEP YOUR WAY." The words directed at Kujo were simple, yet full of feeling.

Kujo saw Watari in the figure of L standing before her. The smile of the man, whose existence she had been trying to put out of her mind, was revived. The warm smile he had greeted her with when she had closed herself off from the world in the wake of her parents' deaths.

"Even after you left Wammy's, Watari refused to give that designation to anyone else. Do you intend to denigrate the letter assigned to you by having it stand for 'Killer'?"

Kujo let go of Maki. The doctor looked defenseless, as though all of the armor around her had fallen away.

Suddenly someone jumped at L from behind, tackling him to the ground. "Give it to me!" Matoba cried. He scrambled for the antidote in L's hand, and ate a kick from L's shoe.

"So you value your own life even after you tried to annihilate Japan."

"Shut up!"

The two crashed into the seats as they wrestled each other in the narrow aisle. Matoba mounted L, landed a hard punch to L's jaw, and wrested the ampule away from him.

"Not so fast." L was looking not up at Matoba but over the assailant's head. One of the overhead compartments had popped open. A large attaché case fell from it and slammed down, corner first, on Matoba's head. The syringe fell out of his hand and rolled toward Maki.

"Maki, inject yourself with the antidote now!" L shouted.

Suddenly the airplane swerved off course, sending Kujo tumbling to the floor next to Maki's feet. Maki hesitated for an instant and then snatched up the ampule and injected Kujo with the antidote.

"Maki. Why?" Kujo stared at the mark left on her skin, her mouth hanging open.

"You're the same as my father, Dr. Kujo."

"The same?"

"My father used to dream about his research helping everyone in the world be happy. But he worried that things didn't go the way he wanted. You're the same way. You aren't a bad person after all." Maki smiled. Her gentle smile shook Kujo's soul stained with vengeance and hatred more than anything Maki could have said.

"Don't you hate me for killing your father?"

Maki looked away for a moment, her facial expression turbulent. Then she said, "We have to help the people who are suffering right in front of us no matter who that person may be. And more people can be saved if you survive. I'm the one who should die, to save everyone else."

"You still believe in me, even after I tried to wipe out the people of the world?"

Maki smiled, and a bloody tear rolled down her cheek. "My father used to tell me that no one was born bad. People can…always… change…" Maki faded and fell unconscious.

Kujo could do nothing but hold Maki in her arms and break down in bloody tears of her own.

Matoba, who had been struck dumb after the only antidote was taken away from him, snatched a baby out of the arms of the woman sitting nearby. The mother howled and scratched at Matoba, but he kicked her to the floor. "You won't get in my way any longer, L! If you want to save this child's life, bring me the antidote now. You must have another somewhere!" As the scar on his cheek twitched, a smile as wide and wicked as that of a shinigami crept across his face. "The earth will be a hell when this child grows up. He's better off dying now."

"Dr. Kujo, please stop him," L urged.

"Mr. Matoba, you must stop toying with the future of mankind."

"Shut up, Kujo!"

The plane tried to rise into the sky and shuddered. Wind whipping through the cabin pinned Matoba, L, and Kujo against chair backs and the floor of the aisle itself.

In the cockpit, Fairman cursed, "Shit! I can't take her up with the emergency exit open!" He slammed a fist against the control yoke. "No choice but to move onto Plan G." Fairman scanned the runway in search of something and gripped the yoke.

The plane veered off course, and the cabin shook violently. Losing his balance, Matoba grabbed the edge of the door with one hand and kept the baby clutched in the other.

The plane's rear wheel rode up against a light fixture along the runway, shaking the cabin again. Matoba tumbled from the airplane, the baby still in his arm. Amidst the mother's scream drowning in the turbulence, Kujo beat L to the door. Kujo jumped from the plane and seized the baby from Matoba's hands. She angled herself expertly and rolled, shoulder first, to the ground, cradling the baby in her arms. Suruga, still pinned to the wing and hanging on to the flap with a death grip, could only watch the young woman flash by his eyes, babe in arms.

The precious life in Kujo's arms laughed as it reached out with its tiny arms toward Kujo, unaware of the danger it had been in. *Am I still able to feel something for an innocent life?*

Less gracefully, Matoba bounced off the roof of the takoyaki truck, smacked against the hard concrete and tumbled down the runway. Matoba, his body broken and limbs twisted, couldn't even raise his head. But he could smile and say, "Checkmate, L."

Suruga, who had climbed onto the wing of the plane after L, held on as the plane's landing gear once again hit the runway and finally managed to pull himself to the cabin door. Rushing inside he shouted, "Ryuzaki, we've got trouble! They're trying to crash this plane into a refueling truck!"

"Mr. Suruga, the cockpit!"

"Right!"

Suruga drew his gun, drilled a bullet into the lock, and kicked down the cockpit door. "Fairman! We have a score to settle!" He immediately shot Fairman in the thigh, and before he could let out a sound, kneed him in the jaw, knocking him unconscious. Suruga was actually showing mercy—he wanted to spare Fairman the pain. Entering the cockpit, L jumped into the pilot's seat and punched the switches on the console in an attempt to cut the engine.

Outside, Matsuda had driven the takoyaki truck toward the refueling truck and was scrambling to move it out of the way. But neither the key nor driver was anywhere to be found. "What'll I do..." He jumped back into the takoyaki truck, pointed it directly at the airplane streaking toward him, and slammed down on the accelerator. He screeched to a halt just in front of the airplane's landing gear and flung himself out of the truck.

"Stop!" L, Suruga, and Matsuda yelled at once.

The enormous front wheel of the plane collided with the truck. The vehicle was pushed backward by the overwhelming momentum of the massive aircraft. There was the crunch of metal as the plane's wheel rolled up the hood of the truck and crushed it. The plane slowed down slightly, but it was enough. UA Flight 718 bumped its nose against the tank of the refueling trunk and rolled to a halt.

†

A VTOL fighter jet touched down on the runway, which had been shut down and cordoned off by an alphabet soup of law enforcement and public health authorities.

"It appears you made it in time," L said.

The canopy popped open and out crawled Takahashi from the rear seat of the fighter. "Ryuzaki, you sent this thing to land right in front of my house! Blew off roof shingles all over the neighborhood!" He dug into his medical bag. "Here's what you asked for."

"You've done it. Thank you."

Following L's instructions, the flight attendants inoculated the panic-addled passengers aboard the plane. Kujo was sitting slumped in the aisle.

"Dr. Kujo, please inoculate Maki with the antidote." L handed Kujo an ampule. "Dr. Kujo—no, I shall call you K—people are indeed foolish. But they also have the capacity to change. Don't you believe the world can change if children with a sense of justice, like Maki, are allowed to grow up with their innocence untouched?" The same watchful eyes that had looked over Maki were now directed at Kujo.

Such strong, kind eyes...

Overwhelmed by the sure hope imbued in L's eyes, Kujo had no choice but to recognize her defeat. The countless setbacks, loneliness, and despair. L exuded the gentleness and steely resilience of someone who had surmounted such obstacles and continued to follow the path in which he believed.

"Dr. Kujo...even a genius cannot change the world alone. It isn't for us to change the world. We can only aid that process. When you have paid for your sins, please use your abilities to help children like Maki."

Kujo simply nodded. Of course, she could not know L had only

two days left to live. Nevertheless, she could sense that something precious was being entrusted to her.

Kujo gave Maki the shot and broke down in tears.

"It was Maki who taught me what I should do in this situation." L knelt down and held both Kujo and Maki in his arms. He stroked their heads gently. "You did well. You're both going to be all right."

†

The police were taking the Blue Ship members into custody, a long line of misguided idealists now hunched over and hiding their faces in shame.

"Our job is done here, Watari. Now, how about something sweet—" L spoke to a man who was no longer at his side. It had been customary for Watari to bring him a previously unsampled confection on a silver tray after the completion of a mission. "No... perhaps not."

L watched Kujo being taken away in handcuffs. Kujo walked, head high, looking directly ahead, as if she were setting her sights on a new path she had recently discovered. For L, it was a sight sweeter than any dessert that might have been brought to him at that moment.

"Watari, I think I'd like to stay here a while longer."

The pilot of the fighter jet held out a laptop in front of L and opened it.

"I'm glad I was able to assist you, L," said a synthetic voice. "The answer to the puzzle will be made public in two days."

"No doubt the United States will be put in a difficult situation. Perhaps it will ease Dr. Kujo's mind a little."

L looked at the computer screen. Only the letter "N" was floating onscreen.

"Thank you, Near."

L 00-1 Reunion

When Maki opened her eyes, she was inside a hospital room. She lay in a bed sealed off from the world by an isolator tent.

"I'm alive?" She could only remember fragments of what had gone on inside the plane because of the high fever brought on by the virus. But there was one memory she could clearly recall. It was the image of L, who despite all his cuts and scrapes, had saved her just as he had promised.

"Everything is going to be all right, Maki." Three figures in hazmat suits were looking at her from the other side of the tent. Though they wore goggles, Maki recognized the smiling faces of Suruga and the Takahashis.

"Where is Ryuzaki?"

"He's gone, " Suruga answered. "He had one last job to do."

"Oh…"

Suruga stood by the window and looked out in the direction of Tokyo. "Ryuzaki's an idiot. Making up some story about a Death Note and fake L. Worrying about the world after he's gone."

And about me…

L had brought an unexpected proposition to Suruga, who was no longer employed by the FBI. He recalled L's last words:

"Mr. Suruga, while it is possible for Wammy's to provide for you financially for the remainder of your days, that isn't what you want, is it? Which is why I am offering you another job. Will you work with N of Wammy's House? Your field skills will be of great help to N."

"Who is N?"

"He is called Near, or Next. 'Near' as in the one soon to follow after L, and 'Next' as in the one to succeed L. He may be a touch more difficult to handle than I was…"

Afterward, L had taken out a Chupa Chups from his pocket and handed it to Suruga along with an official invitation.

"What was the last job Ryuzaki had to do?" Maki asked.

Suruga peered into Maki's eyes through his goggles. "To make certain that children like you can go on smiling in this world. By the way—" Suruga held a baseball up to the glass. "A present from Ryuzaki." It was autographed—a Tigers ball? Maki perked with excitement. But it was a ball signed by Ryuzaki:

"How are you, Maki? See you soon."

The instant she saw the message, Maki knew that she would never see Ryuzaki again. Ryuzaki, who dropped crumbs everywhere when he ate sweets while perched atop the sofa. Who bit his fingernails as he walked with rounded shoulders. Who risked his life to protect her. The Ryuzaki she adored.

"Your jokes are getting better, Ryuzaki."

Maki looked through the isolator and out the window at the twilight sky. She smiled as her eyes welled up with tears. She knew she had to live to change the world. The way her father and L had wanted, the way they had done so.

L00-2 Friend

Twenty days had passed since the Kira investigation had closed, and Soichiro Yagami had resumed his normal duties at the police force. Returning from a day on the job, Soichiro handed his wife Sachiko his jacket and bag, and went straight to the family altar to put his hands together before Light's funeral picture.

Friends from Light's high school and college days had visited daily to pay their respects following his death. Light's smiling face was surrounded by the flowers left around the altar.

"Light was murdered by Kira..." That was the sad lie Soichiro had told both Sachiko and his daughter Sayu. But at that moment, he believed it. That Light had truly been killed by Kira. Light had wanted to protect the happiness of his loved ones. That was why he had taken the Death Note in his hands and sought to right the world by cleansing it of evil people. Why he had succumbed to the temptation of the Kira in everyone's soul.

"A kind society; what Dad desired," Light used to say.

Only three weeks had passed since the killings had ceased, and crime rates had climbed back up to where they had been in the pre-Kira era. The calls for Kira's resurrection accompanied every new bloody spectacle of murder and thievery.

Soichiro had been made to know how powerless "justice under law" was, how it existed only in principle. Even so, he had denied Kira—he had forsaken Light, his own son. As a detective, as Light's father, and as a human being.

"Did Light's friends visit again today?" he asked, noting the offerings left in front of Light's picture.

Sachiko stuck her head out from the kitchen and answered, "Yes, a friend from Light's university. He—what was his name, Sayu?"

"What was it? He was kind of a strange man. But maybe he's the type to get along with Light."

Sachiko and Sayu played at good cheer, which pained Soichiro all the more. "No, I think I know." Placed at Light's altar were five manju skewered on a stick.

"Sorry, Sachiko, Sayu. I'm going out again."

Soichiro put on the jacket he'd just take off and went out again.

"Ryuzaki...you're back."

𝓛 00-3 **Promise**

"Mr. President, this is L."

"Yes..." Although it was the call he had been waiting for, President Hope remained guarded. He could not know which L had called him. Though distorted by a vocoder, the voice sounded reassuring, as if L had anticipated his trepidation.

"The L organization has captured L-Prime and recovered the Death Note. We will eliminate L-Prime with the notebook. You can confirm the body in one hour at the Kira Investigation Headquarters in Japan."

"Then the Death Note?"

"It will be locked away by the L organization, never to be used again. I urge you and future presidents to be mindful of this."

"I understand." The president could not answer otherwise. Although the president's best-case scenario would have been L's elimination, and for the United States to claim possession of the Death Note, he had to be satisfied with being able to confirm the death of the L who had been threatening him.

L's voice took on a mischievous tone. "By the way, Mr. President, would you mind if we also issued you a threat?"

"What is the meaning of this, L?" The president sprang to his feet.

The worst-case scenario spelled out by the FBI suddenly flooded his mind.

"You will ensure a future where children can go on smiling. Will you promise us that? If you should break that promise, we will not hesitate to use the Death Note."

The synthetic effect of the vocoder had dropped away. The president heard L's real voice for the first time. It was different than what the president had expected. Aloof, yet innocent and childlike. The proud voice of someone who refused to lose hope while bearing the burden of protecting justice. The voice of a lonely youth calling from a desolate wasteland. A gentle, hopeful voice hinting at an inner power that only someone who still believed in both strength and kindness could have.

With the greatest expression of respect for the voice he heard, and for what he heard in that voice, the president said, "All right. You have my word, L."

L00-4 Journey

When Soichiro Yagami exited the Kira Investigation Headquarters, Matsuda ran toward him. "I heard Ryuzaki was back."

"Let him be. It's time."

Matsuda bit his lip, nodding sadly, and looked up at the sky. "Ryuzaki..." Matsuda turned to the Kira Investigation building and saluted. It was the best parting gesture he could give to a brother in arms.

†

L was perched on the sofa, his legs folded against his chest as usual. Tossing the cell phone marked "President of the United States" into the trash, he took out a chocolate bar Maki had given him.

"Maki, are you waking up about now? Make your day be a good one."

L took off the wristwatch that was a memento of Light and placed it next to the picture of Watari.

"Light, I'll see you on the other side. Let us explore the world of nothingness together."

As he nibbled on the chocolate bar, L continued to play chess alone. But perhaps his opponent was visible to L.

"Watari, it's been a while since we played chess."

"Finally, we can take our time."

"Since I was a child, I have never beaten you at chess."

"That's right. And I won't go easy on you today."

The sound of the pieces being moved on the chessboard echoed inside L's suite. It was a warm, familiar sound, like a duet played between two men who understood each other.

L looked up suddenly and gazed at Watari's photo with the worried expression of a child. "Watari, have I fulfilled your expectations?" Watari answered with his usual serene smile and uttered one simple unerring word: "Fully."

L smiled an innocent smile. Watari slid his knight in front of L's king.

"L, checkmate."

In a kind and comforting voice, Watari announced the time.

Author's Note

I am deeply grateful to writer Hiroto Kawabata and Toshihiko Komatsu of the NPO Biomedical Science Association for their invaluable guidance.

This work is a novel adaptation of the film *L, Change the WorLd* as well as an homage to the original comics, novel, and live-action films that preceded it. While it is loosely connected with the previous works, I hope you'll enjoy reading this novel as an L story from an alternative continuity.

M

Profile of M

Age and gender undisclosed.
Highly regarded as a cutting-edge writer with bold
ideas and sure-handed storytelling technique. Took
part in "The L Project" after being approached by
the producer, who took notice of M's work.

Original concept by Tsugumi Ohba•Takeshi Obata
First appeared in the January 2008 issue of *Shosetsu Subaru*.